The Case of
the Twin Teddy Bears

Nancy glanced out the door of the toy shop. The storefront lights illuminated the falling flakes, and the streets were quiet.

Suddenly a scream from outside shattered the stillness. Startled, Nancy swung her gaze to Bess, then Dotty, the store owner. "Did you hear that?" Nancy asked.

Reacting quickly, Nancy threw open the front door. Bess called out, "Be careful!" as Nancy dashed out.

Then Nancy heard another scream. With a pounding heart, she ran through the blinding snow toward the cry. It had come from her right, but she couldn't see anyone. Then she spotted a figure sprawled on the ground.

"Are you all right?" Nancy cried out. Reaching the person, Nancy crouched down. From beneath a coat hood, a girl's frightened face looked up at her.

Nancy Drew
Mystery Stories

Available from Simon & Schuster

NANCY DREW® 116

THE CASE OF THE TWIN TEDDY BEARS

CAROLYN KEENE

Aladdin Paperbacks
New York   London   Toronto   Sydney   Singapore

This book is a work of fiction. Any references to historical events, real people, or real locales are used fictitiously. Other names, characters, places, and incidents are the product of the author's imagination, and any resemblance to actual events or locales or persons, living or dead, is entirely coincidental.

First Aladdin Paperbacks edition May 2002
First Minstrel edition December 1993

Copyright © 1993 Simon & Schuster, Inc.
Produced by Mega-Books of New York, Inc.

ALADDIN PAPERBACKS
An imprint of Simon & Schuster
Children's Publishing Division
1230 Avenue of the Americas
New York, NY 10020

Printed in the United States of America

20 19 18 17

ISBN 0-671-79302-0

Contents

THE CASE OF THE
TWIN TEDDY BEARS

1

A Scream in the Snow

"Don't tell me it's snowing again," Bess Marvin grumbled to Nancy Drew. When Bess swung open the front door of Beary Wonderful, snowflakes swirled into the small shop.

"It sure is," Nancy said as she entered the store where Bess worked part-time. Pulling off her snow-covered cap, Nancy shook free her reddish-blond hair. "The weather report predicted seven inches."

Bess shivered as a blast of cold air followed Nancy inside. "That's too cold for me," Bess said, shutting the door. "I'm ready for spring."

Nancy laughed as she dusted a sprinkling of snowflakes off her coat sleeves. Bess was definitely not the outdoor type. That was one of the reasons she hadn't gone on the cross-country ski trip with her parents, her cousin George Fayne, and George's family. The other reason was that the

1

holiday shopping rush was keeping her busy at the store.

"So this is Beary Wonderful?" Nancy asked, looking around.

"Yup, this is Beary Wonderful," Bess said proudly. Throwing her arms wide, she gestured to the shelves and tables decorated for Christmas with stuffed animals, dolls, and handcrafted toys. Dotty Baldwin, the shop's owner, was known for her high-quality new and antique toys.

"Dotty has a super selection for the holiday," Bess added. Taking Nancy's elbow, Bess led her to the back corner of the shop. "These are the teddy bears I was talking about."

Nancy stopped to admire the whimsical display Dotty had set up. In the center of a round table a foot-high bear dressed as Santa Claus was seated at a child's desk, writing out his Christmas list. Clustered around him, three-inch bears in elf suits busily made tiny toys.

"They're so *cute!*" Nancy exclaimed. "I can see why you've fallen in love with them, Bess." Reaching out, Nancy flipped over the price tag hanging from an elf bear.

Nancy gasped and said, "A hundred and twenty-five dollars? Isn't that expensive for a kid's toy?"

Bess shook her head emphatically. "These aren't kids' toys. They're collector bears." Picking up the elf, she showed Nancy a little booklet attached to the bear's side. "Each one is hand-

2

made by a bear artist. Only a limited number are crafted. So someday this little guy will be worth a fortune."

"You hope," Nancy said, her blue eyes twinkling. Since Bess had started working at Beary Wonderful, she'd already bought several teddy bears for "investments," thinking that in the future they'd be worth lots more than what she'd paid for them.

"Oh, they will be." Bess tossed her blond hair behind her shoulder. "Just look at this." She pointed to a glass-enclosed display counter at the back of the shop. The computer register was perched on top. "This is Dotty's personal collection. Some of her bears are worth *thousands*."

Bending over, Nancy peered into the lighted case. About fifteen teddy bears were arranged on red velvet fabric, surrounded by sprigs of holly and shiny ornaments.

"See the one in the middle?" Bess said, tapping on the glass in front of a ten-inch bear with pure white fur and wistful brown eyes. A red ribbon was tied in a bow around its neck. "That's Dotty's Happy Birthday Bear. He's worth over eighty thousand dollars!"

"Wow!" Nancy exclaimed. "I know you told me bears are a good investment, but—"

"Was that a customer?" A cheerful voice from behind the counter made Nancy turn. A gray-haired woman bustled in from the back room carrying an armful of dolls.

3

"No, just my friend, Nancy Drew," Bess replied. "Nancy, I'd like you to meet Dotty Baldwin."

"Hello." Nancy smiled. Dotty Baldwin was plump and grandmotherly looking. Her gray hair was permed into tight curls, her wire-rimmed spectacles were propped on her nose, and her shoes were sensible oxfords.

"Hello, Nancy Drew," Dotty said. She began arranging the dolls on chairs around a child's wooden table set for tea. "You must be Bess's detective friend."

"Yes," Nancy replied. "I've been admiring your shop. I can see why Bess has gotten so crazy about teddy bears."

"Though she still doesn't believe me when I say they're a good investment," Bess added huffily.

Abruptly Dotty stopped arranging and peered at Nancy over her glasses. "Oh? Well, maybe I should give you my lecture about toys and bears being the collectibles of the future. Forget painters, like Picasso and Monet." She waved her hand dismissively. "Who wants a canvas covered with lines and squiggles hanging on the wall when you can have a bear!" Dotty picked up a plump brown bear wearing a blue sweater and handed it to Nancy.

Nancy wasn't quite sure what she was supposed to do with it. Bess nudged her with her elbow.

4

"Go ahead, give it a hug," Bess insisted.

Nancy gave the bear a quick squeeze. "That *is* cuddly," she said with surprise.

Dotty nodded. "It's an Otto C. Bear. That's a famous German brand especially made for hugging. They're limited editions—that means the company only makes about a thousand, then gets rid of the pattern. This one sells for a hundred and fifty dollars today. Four years from now you'd be able to sell it at a collectors' show for double its price."

"Wow," Nancy said as she set the bear down. Dotty was definitely persuasive. No wonder Bess had spent most of her month's wages on bears.

"Dotty, tell Nancy about the Happy Birthday Bear," Bess said eagerly. "He's my favorite of them all."

Dotty smiled and a look of bliss swept over her face. "My baby," she crooned as she walked over to the display case. "He's an Otto C. Bear, too—one of the first ever made. This year he's a hundred years old."

"What makes him worth so much money?" Nancy asked, eyeing the ordinary-looking white bear.

"Nancy!" Bess exclaimed, looking shocked at her friend's question. "Just look at his perfect expression—doesn't he look real? His fur is the finest mohair, and every inch of him is hand-stitched. I'd give anything to have him."

Dotty laughed. "What Bess said is true, but

5

there are several other reasons why he's worth so much. One: He was the only one made." Dotty held up her fingers as she ticked off the list. "Two: There's quite a history attached to him. He was given to a German princess for her birthday—that's why he's called the Happy Birthday Bear. And three: He's in 'mint' condition, which means he's just as good as when he was made."

"I see," Nancy said. It was still hard to believe that a stuffed animal could be worth so much. "If he's that valuable, I hope the display case is locked."

"Of course—the insurance company requires that." Dotty pointed to the silver lock hooked on the edge of the sliding glass door. Nancy bent down and saw that it was a type that a thief could easily pick.

"I'm afraid that won't deter a determined burglar," Nancy said.

Dotty nodded in agreement. "That's why I had a security company install a spot protection system. If anyone unlocks, breaks, or opens the cabinet doors, it sounds a shrill alarm that you can hear all over the riverfront. I keep it on all the time."

"I hope you're the only one who knows how to deactivate the security system," Nancy said.

"Yes," Dotty replied. "And I plan to keep it that way. My parents gave me the Happy Birthday Bear for my own tenth birthday, forty-five years ago, so I never want to lose it. And even though the other bears in the case aren't worth as much, they're still rare Schuco, Steiff, and Bing bears."

Bess sighed. "I wish I'd started collecting earlier. Just think of the bears I'd own by now."

"Oh, that reminds me, Bess. I have a surprise for you." Arching her brows, Dotty grinned mischievously at her employee. Then she spun on her flat heels and brushed through the curtained doorway that led to the back room of the shop.

"Oooh—I wonder what it is?" Bess clapped her hands together like a delighted child. "A new shipment of bears just came in this morning. Ingrid unpacked them. Ingrid Jennings is the other girl who works for Dotty."

Nancy couldn't help but laugh as Bess craned her neck and looked anxiously toward the back room. Her friend had really gone bonkers over bears.

"Look what came in the shipment this morning from Germany," Dotty said as she stepped through the doorway. In her arms she cradled a snow-white bear wearing a red ribbon.

Bess's eyes widened and her mouth fell open. "It's the Happy Birthday Bear!" she exclaimed.

"Not *the* Happy Birthday Bear," Dotty corrected her. "It's a replica of the one I own. Otto C. Bears is making a limited number to celebrate their one hundredth anniversary. I ordered several, but this was the only one to come in this month."

7

With her mouth still open, Bess looked into the bear's eyes. "He's beautiful. And he looks just like the real one."

Nancy squinted down into the glass cabinet. The real bear looked up at her with its pensive smile. She had to agree they did look alike.

"He's all yours," Dotty said, handing Bess the replica bear.

"Mine!" Bess's eyes popped even wider as she took the ten-inch bear in her arms. "But if this is the only one, don't *you* want him?"

The shop owner shook her head. "I own more bears than I need," she said, waving her hand at the rows of stuffed animals in the shop.

"I won't be able to pay you all at once," Bess said. Pulling her purse from the counter, she reached in and dug a twenty-dollar bill from her wallet. "But this will be a start."

Dotty took the bill from Bess's fingers. "He costs two hundred and fifty dollars, but don't worry—you can pay me by working extra hours. Ingrid is going to Germany for a week before Christmas, and I'll need you to help with the holiday rush."

"I'll be happy to work every day," Bess said enthusiastically.

"We'd better get going, Bess," Nancy finally said. Bess's Camaro had gone into the garage for transmission work the day before, so Nancy had offered to pick Bess up after work. "I've got new snow tires, but I still want to get home before the roads get too slippery."

Dotty went over to the shop's front door. "Ingrid said she was going to stop in for her paycheck. I wonder if she decided not to."

Nancy glanced out the door. The storefront lights illuminated the falling flakes. The shop was in the newly renovated waterfront section along the Muskoka River. Small shops and boutiques lined one side of the road. Across the street was the Riverside Restaurant and the Scene, a successful nightclub. But right now the streets were quiet. Nancy figured the prediction of snow had kept many people home.

Suddenly a scream from outside shattered the stillness. Startled, Nancy swung her gaze to Bess, then Dotty.

"Did you hear that?" Nancy asked. By the surprised expressions on their faces, she knew they had heard the scream, too.

Reacting quickly, Nancy threw open the front door and dashed onto the sidewalk. She heard Bess call out, "Be careful."

· Streetlights glowed above, but still it was hard to see. Then Nancy heard another scream. With a pounding heart she ran through the blinding snow toward the cry.

2

Bears, Bears, Bears

Cold, wet flakes pelted Nancy's face as she raced down the icy sidewalk. The scream had come from her right, but she couldn't see anyone. Then she spotted a figure sprawled on the ground.

"Are you all right?" Nancy cried out. Reaching the person, Nancy crouched down. A girl's frightened face looked up at her from beneath a coat hood.

"Yes!" the girl replied breathlessly as she struggled to her knees. Nancy grasped her elbow and helped her to her feet. "I was grabbed," the girl explained, "from behind. I screamed and hit out, but then I slipped on the snow and fell."

The girl bent down to brush away the slush clinging to her coat and jeans. Nancy noticed large footprints in the snow, leading between two buildings and into a parking lot.

Bess dashed up. "Are you guys okay? Ingrid!" she exclaimed when she saw the girl. "What happened?"

"You two go back to the shop," Nancy said quickly. "I'm going to follow these tracks."

"No!" Ingrid grabbed Nancy's arm. "You might get hurt."

Nancy gave her a reassuring smile, then took off down the alley. She didn't want to waste time explaining to Ingrid that she was an experienced detective who had been in lots of dangerous situations.

The footprints were wide apart, as if the person had been running. Nancy followed them to the large parking lot behind the row of shops. A sudden movement at the far side of the lot caught her eye. Someone jumped into a dark-colored car and slammed the door. Then Nancy heard the motor roar.

She ran toward the car, but it zoomed from the parking space. Skidding on the snow, it raced out of view. Disgusted, Nancy kicked the snow. If she'd only been a second earlier, she could have at least seen the car's license plate number. But she did notice that the person was tall—too tall to be a woman, she decided. When she compared her footprint to one of the tracks, she could see that the other person's foot was much larger than hers.

Bending down, she inspected the print closer.

The sole of the shoe or boot had pressed a diamond-grid pattern in the snow. She would have to point that out to the police.

When Nancy got back to the shop, Ingrid had pulled off her hood. Dotty was handing her a cup of steaming cocoa. Bess was looking down worriedly at her.

"I followed your attacker," Nancy said to Ingrid. "Unfortunately, he got away. And I didn't even get a license plate number."

"That's too bad." Ingrid looked up from her hot drink. She had long blond hair pulled back with two barrettes. Her pretty face was still red from the cold. Nancy noticed she spoke with a slight accent.

"I don't even know if it *was* an attacker," Ingrid admitted. "He might have just bumped into me—maybe I panicked and slipped on the ice."

Nancy furrowed her brow. "I don't think so. He sure took off running—that doesn't sound like an innocent bystander to me. I think we'd better call the police. There were some interesting footprints they'll want to see. The sole made a pattern in the snow."

"I'll call and report it." Dotty reached for the phone beside the computer register.

Ingrid jumped up, and said, "Don't bother." Then she smiled sheepishly. "I didn't even see the person. It was dark, and he came up behind

12

me. I *thought* someone grabbed me—that's why I screamed. But I might have been confused." She chuckled. "That's probably why he took off—all that yelling scared him."

Bess frowned. "I don't know, Ingrid. It might have been a mugger."

Ingrid waved her hand. "Look, if I make a report, the police will want me to hang around. But next Sunday I'm headed back to Germany for the holidays. I've saved all fall for this trip, and I don't want it ruined."

Ingrid's reasons made sense, Nancy thought. Still . . .

"Well, the most important thing is you're all right," Dotty said, placing the phone back on the hook.

"Thanks to . . ." Ingrid started to say something, then she spotted the replica Happy Birthday Bear leaning against the register. "What's he doing out here? I didn't put a price tag on him yet."

"So that's why you'd tucked him away in the back corner," Dotty said, reaching for the bear. "I found him this evening when I was looking for more gift boxes. I hadn't realized he'd been delivered already."

"Yes. I unpacked him earlier," Ingrid explained. "But the shop was so busy I didn't get to tag him and put him out."

"And I'm glad, because guess what?" Bess

13

asked, taking the bear in her arms. "Dotty sold him to me! She says she has enough bears, so I can add him to my collection. Isn't that wonderful?"

Ingrid looked surprised. "B-but I was hoping to buy him for my cousin, Karl, in Germany," she stammered. "His birthday is right before Christmas."

"Ingrid's mom is German," Dotty explained to Nancy. "Her dad's American, but he was in the military, so their family has lived in Germany most of her life. When her father retired this year, they came back to the States." She turned back to Ingrid. "Why don't you buy Karl one of these cute Christmas bears? He'd probably like it better."

Ingrid bit her lip. "Well . . . I had my heart set on the Happy Birthday Bear. It just seemed right."

Nancy looked over at Bess. She was hugging the bear tight, an anxious expression on her face. Nancy could tell that her friend was weighing the idea of giving the bear to Ingrid.

"I'm sorry," Dotty said. "I ordered several, but only a limited number are sent to the States, so it could be a month before I get another one. Wait!" She snapped her fingers. "I know what I can do."

Moving behind the counter, Dotty picked up the phone. "I'm sure Arnold Smythe at Totally Toys ordered some."

She punched in the numbers, then waited. "Arnold? It's Dotty. Glad I caught you."

While Dotty talked, Nancy unbuttoned her coat. She'd gotten hot from running. Ingrid was quietly sipping her cocoa, while Bess cradled the bear.

"It's all set," Dotty declared when she hung up. "Arnold received one yesterday, and he'll be happy to save it for you, Ingrid."

"But his shop is in Ardmoore," Ingrid said. "Isn't that an hour from here?"

Dotty nodded. "Not to worry. Write me a check, and I'll have Larry pick up the bear in the morning. You'll have your bear by the afternoon."

Ingrid smiled. "Okay. And thanks." She set down the cup. Then she picked up her purse and rummaged through it for her checkbook. "By the way, Dotty, I need my paycheck."

"Oh, right," Dotty chuckled. "After you came all the way out here in the snow, it would be a shame to forget it." She went into the back room.

Bess grinned at Ingrid. "That's great—we'll both have our bears."

"Yeah." Ingrid smiled back at Bess, but Nancy thought it seemed kind of forced. Ingrid obviously didn't want to wait for another bear.

"You're going back to Germany for Christmas?" Nancy asked her.

Ingrid nodded. "Most of my friends and relatives live there, and I really miss them."

"How long have you been here?" Nancy asked.

"Since the summer," Ingrid said. "I just finished college in Germany, then I came back to live with my folks. I've been pretty lonely, though. I was really glad when Dotty hired me this fall." She laughed. "I'm a bear collector, too. I guess I hung around the store so much, Dotty took pity on me and hired me."

Dotty came out and handed Ingrid her paycheck. "So who's working tomorrow?" she asked the girls.

"You are," they both chorused, looking pointedly at the shop owner.

Dotty rolled her eyes. "That's right. Well, Tuesdays are always slow, and with the snow I doubt we'll have many customers. Ingrid, why don't you come by in the evening and pick up your bear? I'll probably close around six."

"Okay."

"Let me get my coat," Bess said. Nancy slipped on hers, and she and Ingrid started slowly toward the front door.

"Hey, why don't you have dinner with Bess and me tomorrow night?" Nancy suggested. "We can take you to the local hangout and introduce you to some of our friends. There will be lots of college kids around during the holidays. A good friend of mine, Ned Nickerson, will be home in a couple of days."

"Ned's just a friend?" Bess said as she came from behind the counter.

Nancy blushed. "Well . . ." She knew Bess was teasing her because Ned was really her boyfriend.

"I'd love to have dinner with you guys." Ingrid's expression brightened. "It's hard to make new friends."

"We'll pick you up around five," Bess suggested. "Then we can stop by the shop with you to pick up your bear."

The three of them waved goodbye to Dotty, then stepped out into the snow. Nancy and Bess walked Ingrid to her car, then went on to Nancy's Mustang.

"I hope it wasn't a mistake not alerting the police," Nancy said to Bess.

"Oh, it'll be fine," Bess said. "In this crazy weather the guy might've mistaken Ingrid for someone he knew. Maybe he was sneaking up to surprise her, and when she started screaming, he freaked out and ran. I know *I* would have."

"Yeah, I guess," Nancy said, unlocking the car door. She just hoped Bess was right.

"Hmmm. That's funny," Nancy said to Bess and Ingrid when they pulled up in front of Beary Wonderful. "The closed sign is on the door already, but it's only five-thirty."

"Dotty probably closed early because there weren't any customers," Bess said from the back seat of Nancy's Mustang. "I mean, the street's practically deserted. Not everyone is brave enough to drive in the snow like you, Nancy."

Ingrid opened the car door. "Let me jump out

17

and see if she's still there. Otherwise, I can get my bear tomorrow."

Nancy put a hand on Ingrid's arm. "Wait a second. Something doesn't look right. Doesn't Dotty keep an outside light on all the time?"

Ingrid nodded. "That's right. When I close up, she always tells me to switch it on."

Nancy slid out of the driver's seat. A chill wind was blowing, and she wrapped her coat tighter around her.

"Hey, I'm coming with you!" Bess shouted as she jumped out of the backseat.

Quickly Nancy strode around the front of the Mustang to the shop's door. She turned the knob. "It's not locked," she said in surprise.

"That's weird," Ingrid said. She was right behind Nancy. "When Dotty puts the closed sign out, she always locks the door."

Bess grabbed Nancy's arm. "Let's call the police," she whispered urgently.

"Let's look around first," Nancy suggested. "Maybe Dotty's working in the back room and just forgot to lock the door. Or maybe someone called while she was closing up and distracted her or . . ." Nancy's voice died as she pushed open the door. She had a nagging fear that Dotty hadn't done any of those things.

The three girls stood frozen in the open doorway. Without the outside light the shop was dark and shadowy. Bess gripped the back of Nancy's arm as she and Ingrid followed Nancy toward the computer register.

"I'll go turn on the lights," Ingrid whispered.

"No," Nancy said. "We stay together until we find out what's going on." She reached in her purse for her pocket flashlight. After turning it on, she swung it around the shop. Dolls and bears grinned at her as the beam flickered over their faces. She aimed the light toward the counter and the cash register.

"Nothing looks out of place," Bess said. "Wait!" She pointed to the floor in front of the counter. A red Christmas ball lay shattered on the carpet.

Lowering the flashlight, Nancy ran the beam along the carpet, then up to the red velvet-covered shelves of the locked case. Behind her Ingrid and Bess gasped. The ornaments glittered in the light, but the rest of the case was empty.

Dotty's valuable bears were gone!

3

Dotty's Dilemma

"All of Dotty's bears are gone!" Nancy cried as she stooped next to the display case.

Bess grabbed Ingrid's arm. "Even the Happy Birthday Bear is gone!" she exclaimed. "The original!"

"The glass doors are open," Nancy said. "I wonder if the alarm went off. Bess, you and Ingrid turn on the shop lights, then call Dotty. I'm going to look in the back."

"You be careful," Bess called as Nancy went behind the counter.

Brushing aside the curtain, Nancy stepped into the dark storeroom. She groped along the wall until she found a light switch.

When the light came on, Nancy could see that the small room was filled from top to bottom with boxes, bags, and trash. In the back left-hand corner was a closed door. Probably an office, Nancy thought.

Carefully Nancy wound her way through the piles and opened the office door. When she turned on the light, Nancy gasped. Dotty was slumped on the floor, wedged between a desk and a swivel chair. Her eyes were closed.

Nancy knelt down to feel the woman's pulse.

"There's no answer at Dotty's . . . oh, no!" Bess cried as she came up behind Nancy. "Is she all right?"

Nancy nodded. "Her pulse is strong," she said. Gently she examined Dotty's head and neck. "And there doesn't seem to be any injury, but I can't be sure."

Just then Ingrid came through the doorway. "There's no sign of the bears anywhere," she said. But she stopped dead when she saw Dotty. "Oh, no!" Ingrid said, then clapped her hand to her mouth.

"Ingrid, call nine-one-one," Nancy said firmly. "Tell them what happened."

Without another word Ingrid disappeared into the front room.

Bess stooped down next to Nancy. "What do you think happened?" she asked. She took off her coat and laid it over Dotty. The shop owner groaned.

"I'm not sure." Raising her head, Nancy sniffed the air. "Do you smell something sweet?"

21

Bess sniffed, too. "Yeah—what is it?"

"My guess is that Dotty was chloroformed," Nancy replied. "She'll be all right. Why don't you get a cool towel to put on her head?"

"Good idea." Bess headed for the bathroom.

"The police and the rescue squad should be here any minute," Ingrid said, returning to the office.

Nancy looked up at her. "When you checked the shop, did you notice if anything else was stolen?" she asked.

Ingrid shook her head. "Just the bears from the locked case. Whoever took them must have known how valuable they were."

Nancy gestured around the office. "How about in here? Is anything out of place?"

Ingrid scooted around Nancy and crossed over to the desk. She pulled out the drawers, then shook her head. "I don't think so, but this is Dotty's office—Bess and I don't have much reason to come back here. Dotty does all the paperwork herself."

"Here's something for her head," Bess said, bringing in a damp towel. "Is she coming out of it?"

Nancy looked back down at the shop owner. Dotty's eyelids fluttered open, then she put a hand on her head and moaned.

"I feel terrible," Dotty groaned. For a second, she stared up at the three girls. Then she struggled to a sitting position and looked around the office, obviously confused. "What happened? What am I doing on the floor?"

Nancy put a gentle hand on Dotty's shoulders. "Easy does it until the medics get here," she said.

"The police should be here any second, too," Bess added.

"Medics? Police?" Dotty's eyes widened. "Will you girls tell me what happened?"

"We're not sure," Nancy said. She told Dotty about finding the front door open, the lights off, the case open, and the bears gone.

Dotty's mouth dropped open. "My antique bears were stolen?" she repeated, stunned.

Ingrid nodded. "Even the Happy Birthday Bear."

With a groan Dotty laid her head back against the side of the desk. "But how?" she wailed. "I was here, and the alarm system was on."

"Dotty, tell us what happened tonight," Nancy said earnestly.

Dotty pressed her fingers to her temples. "I decided to close at five o'clock because business was slow. So I put out the sign and locked the front door."

"You're sure you locked it?" Nancy asked.

Dotty nodded. "And I'm positive about the time, too, because the cuckoo clock in the front rang out five times. I lost my watch yesterday, so I've had to rely on that silly bird all day."

"Good," Nancy said. "These are all details the police will want to hear."

Dotty frowned. "But then I'm not so sure what happened after that. I was standing beside my desk. I was going to call Ingrid and tell her not to come get her bear." She smiled apologetically at Ingrid. "Because of the snowy roads this morning, Larry didn't make it to Ardmoore, so—"

"Dotty," Nancy cut in, trying to get her back on track. "What happened when you went to phone Ingrid?"

"I was reaching for the phone when all of a sudden someone grabbed me from behind, and then . . ." Her voice trailed off. "I don't remember any more."

"You never heard the alarm?" Nancy asked. Dotty shook her head no.

In the distance Nancy heard a siren approaching. A sharp rap on the front door announced the arrival of the police.

Nancy jumped up. "You guys stay with Dotty until the medics arrive."

"Hello," Nancy called as she swept through the curtain into the front. Two officers in uniform stood in the middle of the shop. When Nancy saw the policeman in front, she pulled up short. It was Officer Brody, a member of the River Heights police force. Nancy had worked on two cases with him, but he thought Nancy should leave investigating to the police.

"Well, if it isn't Nancy Drew, Wonder Detective," Brody said sarcastically. "Does that mean you've already solved this crime?"

Before Nancy could reply, two medics charged through the door behind them. "Where's the lady who was hurt?" the taller guy asked.

"Mrs. Baldwin's back here." Nancy led the medics to the back room. "I think she was knocked out with chloroform."

Then Nancy went back to talk to Officer Brody. He was wandering around the shop, tapping a pencil on an opened pad. His partner, Officer Jackson, had her camera out and was taking photographs of the display case.

"So this is the case that was burglarized?" Officer Brody asked Nancy.

"Yes," Nancy replied. "As you can see, it wasn't broken into. Someone was able to pick that lock and the front door lock as well."

"Or someone had the keys," Officer Brody murmured as he wrote something down on his pad.

"It would've taken more than a key to open the case." Nancy explained about the alarm system.

"Hmmm," Brody said. "I'll have to ask Mrs. Baldwin about that. The woman who called nine-one-one"—Brody consulted his notes—"Ingrid Jennings, said there were at least fifteen valuable bears stolen."

Nancy nodded. "I'm sure Dotty has a list and description of them for insurance purposes."

"Any idea how much they were worth?" he asked.

"One of the bears was valued at over eighty thousand dollars," Nancy told him.

Brody stopped writing and looked up at Nancy. Even Officer Jackson lowered her camera.

"Eighty thousand dollars?" Brody repeated. "You're kidding me."

"No. It was a hundred-year-old antique bear," Nancy explained. "It was one of a kind and once belonged to a German princess."

Brody shook his head in disbelief. "A teddy bear would have to be made of gold before I'd pay that kind of money," he said. He started toward the back room. "Officer Jackson, I'm going to interview Mrs. Baldwin, then check out her alarm system. You'd better wait for the lab guys."

Nancy followed Brody to Dotty's office. The shop owner was sitting in the chair, a blood pressure cuff on her arm. Bess stood to one side of the chair, while Ingrid sat on the edge of the desk, out of the medics' way.

"I really feel fine," Dotty insisted as the medics poked and prodded her.

One of them sighed. "You are fine. Though you may have a splitting headache for a couple of days. Chloroform does that to a person."

"Chloroform?" Officer Brody asked with a frown.

The medic nodded toward Nancy. "The young lady mentioned she thought Mrs. Baldwin had been knocked out with a gas. We both smelled the sweetish scent." He closed his bag, then stood up. "But I'm sure your lab guys can get a sample from around her mouth and nose."

Officer Brody nodded. When the medics left, he looked pointedly at Ingrid, Bess, and Nancy. "I'd like you girls to wait in the front of the shop so I can interview Mrs. Baldwin in private," he said. "Then I'll need to speak with each of you."

"Us?" Bess squeaked. "But we haven't had dinner."

"Too bad." Officer Brody dismissed the girls with a wave of his hand.

As she walked back into the front of the shop, Nancy took off her coat. "Brody's just doing his job," she told Bess.

Ingrid sighed as she perched on a stool behind the counter. "It's not like we know what happened."

"Really." Bess removed a giant-size bear from a chair and sat down in its place.

Nancy leaned against the counter and watched Officer Jackson take a shot of the doorknob and lock on the front door. At least they were being thorough, Nancy thought.

The girls must have been waiting for about fifteen minutes when the front door suddenly flew open, letting in a gust of wind. A tall middle-aged man with wild gray-streaked curly brown hair stood in the doorway. His wool coat flapped open, and a red scarf was looped around his neck.

"What's going on?" he demanded, his gaze swinging to Ingrid. "Why is there a cop car out front?"

"Excuse me," Officer Jackson said in a firm voice as she came around the edge of the door. "Who are you and what are you doing here?"

"I'm Larry O'Keefe, and I work for Mrs. Baldwin," he replied. "Where is she? Is she hurt?"

Ingrid jumped up and put her hand on Larry's arm. "Dotty's fine. But there's been a robbery."

"A *what?*" Larry's head snapped around.

Ingrid pointed to the open display case. Larry glanced toward it, then abruptly swung around the counter and headed for Dotty's office.

"Halt!" Officer Jackson ordered. "Officer Brody is interviewing a witness back there."

Larry stopped in his tracks. "I just wanted to see Dotty," he protested. With a worried frown he ran his fingers through his tangled curls. Nancy wondered what his relationship to Dotty was. He certainly seemed concerned.

Officer Brody stepped through the curtained doorway. He fixed Larry with an inquisitive look, then beckoned to Nancy. She followed him into the storeroom. The door of Dotty's office was shut.

"What do you know about Mrs. Baldwin?" Officer Brody asked in a whisper.

Nancy shrugged. "Bess has been working with her since November. She'd be the one to ask."

Brody put a finger to his lips, then leaned closer. "Well, just between you and me, I think I have this case nailed already," he whispered gruffly. "My hunch is that our innocent-looking shop owner stole her own bears!"

4

Shadows and Spies

Nancy was shocked by Brody's accusation. "Why would Dotty steal her own bears?"

"Because she's got them insured for over a hundred thousand dollars," Officer Brody whispered. "She could sell the 'stolen' bears on the black market for a hefty price, then collect insurance money, too."

Nancy frowned and said, "That's ridiculous."

"Look, Detective Drew," he persisted. "Mrs. Baldwin was the only one who knew how to turn that alarm system off. And believe me, that thing is complicated. Maybe a professional thief could've figured it out, but what professional thief is going to steal a bunch of bears?"

"But Dotty was chloroformed," Nancy pointed out.

Brody looked smug. "She could've dabbed

enough on her face to make you think she was gassed."

"I don't believe this is happening." Nancy groaned in frustration. "Why are you telling me all this, anyway?"

"Because you've got a friend working for the lady," Brody said. "She could help us get information."

Nancy frowned. "That sounds like spying. Besides, I like Dotty."

He threw up his hands. "All right. Let her get away with it. Let her—"

"Hey," Nancy interrupted. "You know that if I find out anything that will help you solve this case, I'll let you know."

Officer Brody sighed. "Okay." He flipped open his pad. "Now tell me step by step what happened tonight."

An hour later Brody had finished talking to Bess and was interviewing Ingrid. By that time the lab technicians had arrived, dusted for prints, searched for any other physical evidence, then left.

When Ingrid came back into the front of the shop, Larry was pacing across the room. Nancy, Bess, and even Officer Jackson looked tired and bored.

"So, Mr. O'Keefe," Brody said as he approached the older man. "Where were you this evening and why were you coming back to the store so late?"

For a second Larry appeared to be puzzled. He stopped pacing and stared at Officer Brody.

"Don't worry, he's asking all of us a million questions," Ingrid told him.

"Oh. Well, I had some merchandise to pick up in Bingham," Larry explained. "I left here about four-thirty. The icy roads slowed me down, so I didn't get back until late. I was going to drop off the van out back when I saw the police car."

Officer Brody tapped his pencil on the pad. "Let's see. Bingham's about an hour away. So that means that at the time of the robbery you were on the road."

"I got to the warehouse at Bingham about fifteen minutes before six," Larry added. "You can check with the manager."

"I will." Raising an eyebrow, Brody looked pointedly at Larry. "If we figured the robbery happened at five, then you were the last to see Dotty. Did you notice any strange cars? Anybody hanging around?"

Larry shook his head. "Dotty said she was going to close up early. So I said goodbye and left."

"Well, I think we've got enough," Officer Brody said, flipping shut his pad. Five sighs of relief echoed through the room.

Suddenly Nancy thought of something else. "Officer Brody," she called out. "Let me walk you to your car." Throwing on her coat, she followed the two officers out the front door.

Once outside, Nancy told them all about what happened to Ingrid. Brody frowned, then shrugged.

"It could be related, but I doubt it," he said. "I'll make a note of it in my report. Maybe it was the thief, checking out the shop beforehand."

Nancy arched one brow. "So you admit there's a possibility someone else besides Dotty could've stolen those bears?" she teased him.

He snorted. "A slight one. But no matter what, do me a favor and keep those detective eyes of yours open. And make sure you share everything with me. And I mean *everything*," Brody instructed.

"Will do."

When Nancy went back inside, Dotty had come into the front of the shop. Her face was pale, and she looked older and tired.

Larry came out of the back room with a cup of coffee. "What a creep that cop was," he grumbled to Dotty. "He shouldn't have treated you like *you* were the criminal."

"Don't worry about it." Dotty waved her hand in the air. "Go put the van in the back, then you can drive me home," she told him.

Bess and Ingrid were putting on their coats.

"Are you sure you'll be all right?" Bess asked Dotty.

"I'll open up the shop tomorrow," Ingrid put in. "You don't even have to come in."

Bess added, "I'm not supposed to come in until Thursday, but Ingrid can call if she needs help."

Dotty sighed. "Thanks, girls. You've all been wonderful." She glanced up at Nancy, a worried V between her brows. "May I speak to you a minute?" she asked, motioning her aside.

"Sure." Nancy followed her behind the counter.

"I'm a little worried, Nancy," she whispered. "When Officer Brody was interrogating me, I got the impression he thought I was guilty of stealing my own bears."

Nancy swallowed hard. "I think you guessed right," she agreed.

"Why would he suspect me?" Dotty asked.

Nancy explained Brody's theory about the insurance.

Dotty shook her head emphatically. "Money can *never* replace priceless antiques," she protested. "Plus, several of those bears were my childhood friends. There's no way I'd ever sell them."

"I've got one important question," Nancy said. "Where did you keep the display case key?"

"In my purse, on my key chain," Dotty said. Laying her hand on Nancy's arm, she added, "You're really sharp about this stuff. Will you help me find the real burglar and get my bears back?"

34

"Yes." Nancy gave the shop owner's hand a reassuring squeeze.

Dotty sighed with relief. Nancy buttoned her coat, and the three girls said goodbye.

Fifteen minutes later Nancy, Bess, and Ingrid were in the Marvins' kitchen. It was too late for the dinner out that they had planned, but Bess had invited Ingrid to stay and have a cheese omelet. Nancy was spending the night with Bess, since Bess's parents were gone for the week.

"It's so late my stomach thinks it's time for breakfast," Bess grumbled, pulling a package of shredded cheese from the refrigerator.

Nancy laughed. "It's only eight-thirty."

"I'm hungry, too," Ingrid admitted. "And exhausted." She slumped down on a kitchen chair. "So what did Officer Brody say when you mentioned I'd been attacked last night?" she asked Nancy.

Nancy shrugged. "Not much. He said it was possible your attacker was the burglar. He might have been 'casing' the place—you know, hanging around to find out when the shop closed and who was there at night. But Brody is so convinced that Dotty's guilty, I don't think he'll look into it."

"Well, there's no *way* Dotty's guilty," Bess stated as she slammed the refrigerator door shut.

Nancy didn't reply. She cracked several eggs into a bowl, then whisked them with a fork. She didn't know Dotty as well as Ingrid and Bess did, so it was harder for her to ignore the facts.

"What's with Larry O'Keefe?" Nancy asked the two girls. "He seemed overprotective of Dotty."

"I think he's worked for her a long time," Bess said. Turning on the stove, she began to melt margarine in the omelet pan. "He only works part-time, so we don't see him that much. Only when Dotty needs something picked up or delivered."

"I think she feels sorry for him," Ingrid added.

"Oh?" Nancy glanced over at her, then poured the eggs into the pan.

"I mean, he seems kind of lonely and not too ambitious." Ingrid suddenly stood up. "Hey, is there something I can do?"

Bess pointed to the silverware drawer. "You can set the table. My mom left fruit salad, muffins, orange juice, ham . . . enough food for an army."

An hour later the girls had polished off a late but delicious dinner.

"Let's save the dishes for later," Bess said with a satisfied sigh.

"Ummm. Much later, like tomorrow morning," Nancy said, yawning.

Ingrid glanced at her watch. "Wow—I'd better be heading home. This was really great. Like I said, it's been hard making new friends."

"Why don't you join us for a skating party

tomorrow night?" Nancy suggested. "A bunch of us are going to the park pond."

Ingrid grinned excitedly. "That sounds like fun. I haven't skated in ages. And hey, before I go, Bess, I'd love to see your bear collection."

Bess's eyes brightened. "Sure! I know it's not as big as yours, but Dotty has helped me pick out bears that she knows will go up in value."

"Like the Happy Birthday Bear," Ingrid said, her voice resigned.

Bess's smile fell. "Oh, I forgot—you didn't get yours today. Well, maybe Larry can pick it up tomorrow." She patted Ingrid's arm, then the two girls stood up and went upstairs, chatting excitedly.

Okay, so bears are cute, Nancy thought—but not cute enough to get excited about this late at night. Standing up, she stretched, then carried her dishes to the sink and rinsed them.

When Nancy joined the other two girls ten minutes later, they were perched on Bess's bed, a circle of bears surrounding them. Ingrid was cuddling the Happy Birthday Bear in her arms.

"I guess I'd better say goodbye to him." Ingrid gave the bear one last hug, then stood up.

"I'll drive you home," Nancy offered.

"Oh, I can walk," Ingrid told her. "I only live a block over."

"It's real handy," Bess added. "Ingrid and I have even driven to work together lots of times."

"Great. Then I'll say goodbye now, Ingrid," Nancy said as she opened her overnight bag. "I'm ready for a steaming hot shower."

Waving goodbye, Ingrid followed Bess downstairs.

Nancy pulled out her nightgown and makeup case from her overnight bag. By the time she got out of the shower, Bess was snuggled in bed, sound asleep, her arms wrapped tight around her Birthday Bear.

Nancy couldn't blame her. It had been a long day. Still, as she lay in the twin bed on the other side of Bess's room, she couldn't help but wonder about the robbery at Beary Wonderful. If Dotty wasn't the culprit, who was? And how did the thief know how to turn off the alarm system and unlock the front door?

With those questions floating through her weary mind, Nancy finally fell asleep.

The scream seemed to come from far away. Then the person screamed again. It was louder and more urgent this time.

Nancy struggled awake. Her eyes flew open, and she propped herself up on one elbow. For a second, confusion clouded her brain. Where was she? And who was screaming?

Then she remembered. The Marvins' house. And that was Bess's scream!

Jerking awake, Nancy sat bolt upright. She

could see Bess's shadowy silhouette in the bed next to hers. Her friend was sitting up straight, her bear clutched in one arm.

"Nancy!" Bess cried out, frantically pointing toward the door to the hallway. "Someone's in our house! *Right out there!*"

5

Whose Bear Is Whose?

Nancy's heart flew into her throat. "Someone's in the *hall?*" she asked Bess in a hoarse whisper.

Bess bobbed her head. "I saw a dark shadow moving along the wall. It reached out toward the doorknob, and that's when I screamed."

"I'm going to find out who it is." Flipping back the covers, Nancy swung her bare feet to the floor. She heard a loud thud downstairs. "Call the police!" she shouted to Bess as she ran out of the bedroom.

Quickly Nancy leapt down the steps. Ahead of her, wet splotches dotted the hall carpet. Following them, Nancy sprinted into the kitchen. The back door had been flung wide open.

She dashed onto the back steps. In the pitch black of the night Nancy couldn't see anyone.

On the steps a hodgepodge of footprints led down to the yard. Probably Bess's and Ingrid's,

Nancy decided. But when she stooped, she could make out a much larger print. It had a diamond-grid pattern, just like the tracks in the snow after Ingrid had been attacked.

Nancy flicked on the outside light. The footprints made a trail through the Marvins' backyard, leading to the fence. Had that same person followed Ingrid here? Or was he after someone or something else?

Suddenly Nancy realized her bare feet were numb from the cold. She went back into the kitchen, grabbed a paper towel, and wiped them dry.

"The police will be here any second," Bess said breathlessly as she dashed into the kitchen.

"When Ingrid went out the back door, did the steps have fresh snow on them?" Nancy asked.

Bess nodded yes. "I remember because I told Ingrid to be careful, since they hadn't been shoveled yet."

"Good." Nancy checked the lock on the door. "It doesn't look as if it was forced."

"I'm positive I locked it," Bess insisted.

"Maybe the intruder picked the lock. Come on—we'd better put on robes before the police get here," Nancy said.

Five minutes later the doorbell rang. Nancy opened the door, with Bess right behind her. Officer Brody stood on the front steps, his pad and pencil in hand.

"I thought teenagers got their kicks from going

to the mall or having their hair done," he said in a mocking voice.

"Not us," Nancy said. "We're into more dangerous things like burglars and intruders."

"Intruders, huh?" Brody glanced around curiously as he stepped into the hall.

"Bess woke up and saw someone outside our bedroom door," Nancy explained.

"Male or female?" Brody asked.

Bess shrugged. "It was too dark."

"Then I heard a clunk downstairs," Nancy continued. "When I ran down here, I saw these wet spots in the hall, like snow had melted off someone's shoes. I followed them to the kitchen." She started walking down the hall, with Brody and Bess following.

"The back door was wide open," Nancy explained. "The person ran off before I could catch a glimpse of him. But when I inspected the back steps, I noticed large bootprints leading down into the yard."

"So how do you know an intruder made them?" Brody pointed his pencil at the tracks.

Bess explained how she knew the tracks weren't there earlier. Then Nancy pointed out the pattern in the bootprints and compared them to those in the parking lot the night Ingrid was attacked.

Brody finished writing, then stooped down and studied the back door lock. "It doesn't look broken. Was the deadbolt on?"

"Umm, well." Bess wrung her fingers together. "I forgot to throw the deadbolt, and . . . I think I even forgot to lock the door."

Nancy looked surprised. "But you told me—"

"I know, I know," Bess retorted.

Brody rolled his eyes, then stood up. "I'll have the lab boys check for prints. But I wouldn't bet on finding any. I'll get my camera and take a few shots of the tracks."

"Do you think the two break-ins are related?" Nancy asked as she followed him down the hall.

"Since we don't have a shot of the prints in the parking lot, we can't compare them to the ones in the Marvins' yard," Brody reminded Nancy before he went out to his car.

She dropped her gaze. She knew she should've called the police that night. But Ingrid had been so insistent. Now things were getting complicated, and it was too late to collect what might have been important evidence.

An hour later the police finally left. Nancy carefully checked all the locks, then stumbled upstairs to bed. Bess was snuggled under her quilt, the Happy Birthday Bear tucked beneath her chin. Her eyes were wide open.

"I don't think I'll ever sleep again," Bess said. "I keep seeing a hand reaching for the door-knob." Suddenly she propped herself up on one elbow. "Nancy, will you sleep here all week? Until my parents get home?"

"Sure," Nancy replied as she slid into bed. "Or you can spend the night at my house."

"Good!" Bess sighed dramatically, then flopped back on the bed. "I guess I'll be able to sleep after all."

"Not me." Nancy's mind was racing. She had a hunch there was a connection between the robbery at Beary Wonderful and the break-in at the Marvins' house. But what was it?

"Well, at least they didn't get *my* Happy Birthday Bear," Bess mumbled in a sleepy voice.

The bear! Nancy remembered how the thief had stolen Dotty's valuable bears. Had he been after Bess's, too?

No, that didn't make sense. Shaking her head, Nancy punched her pillow in frustration. The robber had only stolen valuable antique bears.

But what if the robber thought Bess's bear was antique?

"Bess?" Nancy sat up. "Can I see your Happy Birthday Bear for a minute?"

"No! Get your own bear to cuddle," Bess grumbled good-naturedly.

"Come on. This is important."

"Oh, all right." Bess pulled the bear from under the covers and threw it across the space between the two beds. Nancy caught him, then reached up and flicked on the bedside light.

Bess threw the covers over her head.

Holding the bear in two hands, Nancy slowly

turned him around. "How can a person tell your Happy Birthday Bear from the real Happy Birthday Bear?" she asked.

Bess groaned. For a second it was quiet, and Nancy thought she'd fallen asleep. Then the covers flipped back off her friend's face.

"To tell you the truth, I don't know how to tell them apart," Bess said. "But I'm sure an expert can figure it out right away. You'll have to ask Dotty."

"I will." Nancy threw Bess her bear, switched off the light, then plopped back on her pillow.

"So why do you want to know that?" Bess asked.

"I have a theory floating around in my head."

"I should have guessed." Bess sighed. "Okay, so what is it?"

"Maybe the intruder was after your Happy Birthday Bear," Nancy suggested. "What if your bear is the *real* Happy Birthday Bear?"

"Now I know you've really flipped." Bess turned the light back on and stared at Nancy.

"Just listen." Nancy sat up. "What if, for some reason, the antique bear was switched with your bear? The person stashed it back on the shelf, only Dotty found it and sold it to you—not knowing it was the real bear?"

Bess stared at her in disbelief. "Go to sleep, Nancy. You'll be more rational in the morning." Reaching up, she switched the light off.

Nancy blew out her breath. "I guess it does sound kind of crazy. Still, don't you think it's a good idea just to check it out?"

"Mmm-hmm." Bess sounded half-asleep.

"So that's what we'll do tomorrow," Nancy decided. "We won't ask Dotty, since Brody's so sure she's involved. But we could ask the guy who owns that other store, where Larry was getting Ingrid's bear. What was its name?"

There was no answer. "Bess?"

Nancy figured Bess was sound asleep. With a yawn she buried deep under her own covers.

But at least now she had a hunch to act on. And if she was right about the bears being switched, it added a whole new slant to the robbery at Beary Wonderful.

"It still doesn't make any sense," Bess protested the next day as they drove into the town of Ardmoore. She was sitting in the passenger seat of the Mustang, the Happy Birthday Bear perched in her lap. "Why would anyone switch the bears?"

"I haven't figured out the reason yet," Nancy replied as she checked the written directions she'd laid on her lap. The owner of Totally Toys, Arnold Smythe, was meeting them at one o'clock.

"There's the store." Bess pointed down Ardmoore's main street. A wooden bear sign hung outside the shop. Nancy pulled into a parking place in front.

When they pushed open the front door into Totally Toys, a small bell announced their arrival. Nancy had time for a quick glance around the shop, which was full of stuffed animals, wooden toys, dolls, and teddy bears. A short, bald man strode from the back, wearing a striped wool sweater and gray flannel trousers. With his round dark eyes and big ears, he looked like a teddy bear himself.

"Hello, you must be Nancy Drew." He held out pudgy fingers for Nancy to shake.

"Yes," Nancy said. "And this is Bess Marvin. We brought a bear for you to look at."

Bess held out her Happy Birthday Bear. Arnold took it in his hands. "Umm. I have one just like it."

"What we want to know is how you can tell if this is an antique bear," Nancy said.

Arnold's gaze darted from Nancy to Bess. "Did someone sell this to you as a valuable antique?" he asked, his voice suspicious.

"No." Nancy told him about Dotty's bears being stolen. "We just want to make sure this isn't the real bear. We wondered if somehow in the confusion, the thief took the wrong one."

"Dotty's antique bears were stolen!" Arnold gasped. Then he frowned, and a look of suspicion crept into his eyes. "How do I know you girls didn't steal the bears? Now you're trying to find somebody to sell them to."

Bess burst out laughing. "Boy, that's a good one. We're trying to help Dotty."

"Actually, Mr. Smythe has a right to be suspicious," Nancy said. "But you can check with Officer James Brody at the River Heights Police Station."

"Ummm." Arnold grunted, then his scowl melted. "Well, if you're trying to help Dotty, I guess I can look at the bear."

Reaching under his sweater, he pulled half-glasses from a pocket and stuck them on his nose. Then he held the bear up to the light and carefully ran his finger under the eyes. "Nope. This isn't an antique," he said firmly. "Sorry."

"How can you tell so quickly?" Nancy asked.

"Easy." Arnold tapped on one of the bear's eyes. "Feel how warm his eyes are?"

Nancy touched the bear's hard, shiny eyes and nodded.

Turning around, Arnold pulled a ten-inch bear from a high shelf. The bear had a lopsided grin and worn patches in his fur.

"Now, Humpty Bear here is about a hundred years old," Arnold explained. "Feel his eye."

Nancy touched her finger to the smooth surface. "It's cool."

"Right. That's because his eyes—and all the eyes of bears his age—were made of glass. Today all the eyes are made of plastic. Safety codes make it against the law to use glass anymore."

Nancy slowly nodded. Her theory was blown,

but at least she'd learned something to help her identify Dotty's antique bears—if she ever found them.

"Thanks, Mr. Smythe." Nancy shook his hand. "You've been a great help."

"You're welcome." He headed toward the counter. "I'm going to call Dotty and tell her how sorry I am about the theft."

The girls waved goodbye, then slowly sauntered toward the front door. Bess was hugging the Happy Birthday Bear and looking around with interest at the displays of bears. All of a sudden she gasped.

Nancy swung her gaze toward her friend. Bess was crouched in front of a dollhouse. The furniture and accessories were just the right size for the small bears that had been arranged inside the rooms.

"Nancy!" Bess hissed. Reaching up, she grabbed Nancy's wrist and pulled her down beside her. "Look in the kitchen." Bess jabbed her finger toward a small white bear wearing a calico apron. "That's one of Dotty's stolen bears!"

6

Skating on Thin Ice

"Are you sure that's one of Dotty's antique bears?" Nancy asked in a hushed voice. "I mean, they all look alike."

"Yes!" Bess declared firmly.

Nancy looked over her shoulder. Arnold was still talking on the phone. She motioned for Bess to follow her outside.

The door jangled shut, and the two girls hurriedly walked several paces down the street. Then Nancy turned to Bess and asked, "How do you know for sure it was a bear stolen from Dotty's display case and not one of Arnold's?"

"Because of the size and color," Bess explained. "It's a three-and-a-half-inch, white mohair Steiff bear. They're very rare. Dotty showed it to me the other day when business was slow. But what really gives it away is the calico apron. When she was little, Dotty made it for the bear."

Nancy gave a low whistle. "Wow. If you're right, then Arnold Smythe had something to do with the robbery last night. But if he stole the bear, why would he put it in plain sight?"

"Actually, it was pretty well hidden. I only noticed it because it looked so much like Dotty's."

"It would make sense if Arnold was the thief," Nancy said. "He knows the bears are valuable, and I'm sure he knows plenty of people who will buy them with no questions asked. But how did he get into Dotty's display case?"

"He's been in the store before," Bess said. "Sometimes he and Dotty have tea together. Maybe he managed to make a copy of the key somehow."

"That's possible," Nancy said. "And if he wanted those bears badly enough, he could've figured out how to disconnect the alarm. It wouldn't be the first time a clever criminal defeated technology."

Suddenly Nancy inhaled sharply. "Bess, what if Arnold wasn't telling us the truth about *your* bear? If he's the thief, he certainly wouldn't tell us that you have the antique one—he knows we'd give the real Happy Birthday Bear back to Dotty, and she'd put it someplace safe."

"That's right." Bess frowned. "But what about that whole lecture on the glass eyes?"

"He could've made it all up," Nancy reasoned.

Bess sighed. "So what do we do now?"

Nancy thought a minute. "We can't go back in his shop. If Smythe is the thief, he'll get suspicious. We could ask Dotty to confirm or deny what he said about the bear, except . . ." She bit her lip in frustration.

"Except what?" Bess asked.

Nancy looked apologetically at her friend. "Officer Brody considers Dotty the prime suspect. So I have to be careful, too, and not do anything that might jeopardize his case. I'd better call Brody and tell him what's going on. And you'd better hang on tight to that bear."

They located a pay phone in a nearby coffee shop. Brody wasn't on duty yet, so Nancy left a message for him.

"Now what?" Bess asked when they stepped back outside.

Nancy gazed up the sidewalk to Totally Toys. "What I'd like to do is check out the place," she said. "Arnold could have the rest of the bears stashed there."

"Well, don't forget, we're going to that ice-skating party with Ingrid at five," Bess reminded Nancy. "And Ned will be at the party, so you don't want to be late."

Nancy grinned. "Don't worry, I didn't forget. I haven't seen him since Thanksgiving."

"So let's go." Taking Nancy's arm, Bess steered her friend toward the Mustang. "Let's give detecting a rest and let Officer Brody investigate

Arnold Smythe. We've got a skating party to get ready for."

The sun was beginning to set when Nancy finally laced her skates over her heavy socks. She and Bess had picked up Ingrid, then met Ned at the park lake. Though Nancy had been excited to see Ned, she still couldn't get the stolen bears out of her mind.

"Come on, Nancy!" Ingrid skated swiftly past, weaving among the dozen teens already on the ice. "Join the fun."

Nancy waved back. Then she saw Ned zoom toward her from the other side of the park lake. His green ski jacket complemented his eyes, and, without a hat, his brown hair was tousled by the wind and his ears were pink from the cold.

Nancy pulled her knit cap over her reddish-blond hair and stood up from her seat on the log. Several kids were collecting wood to build a fire on the lake shore.

To her left, Nancy could see the parking lot. To her right, picnic tables and a kid's playground were nestled in the pine woods. Beyond that, deeper woods circled the lake.

Nancy hobbled on her blades to the edge of the ice. She hadn't skated since last year, and when she stepped onto the smooth surface, her feet went in all directions.

"Hey!" Ned flew past, doubled back, and took Nancy's elbow. "Need a hand?"

"Thanks!" Nancy laughed, and her breath made smoky clouds in the air. Soon she got her rhythm, and the two sailed over the ice.

"Hey, you two!" Bess skated up behind them about twenty minutes later. "Look what a good skater Bear is."

Holding the Happy Birthday Bear in front of her, Bess circled around them. She was wearing a blue ski jacket and red-striped knit cap. She'd dressed the bear in a doll's sweater and matching knit cap. On his feet he wore tiny ice skates made out of fabric and bent wire.

"Real cute, Bess," Nancy said in a teasing voice. She'd told Bess to make sure she brought the bear so they could keep their eyes on it.

"What's with Bess and that bear?" Ned asked after Bess skated away. "Isn't she a little too old to be taking her stuffed animals out to play?"

Nancy laughed. "Maybe I'd better explain what's going on."

Glancing over her shoulder, she checked to see if anyone was around. They had stopped on the far side of the lake. Most of the other skaters were on the ice near the fire.

In front of Nancy a thick stand of pine trees lined the shore of a hidden cove. On her left side was the parking lot, but she and Ned were too far away for anyone in their cars to hear them.

Turning back to Ned, Nancy filled him in on the robbery and the intruder. She finished by telling him her theory that the intruder had been after Bess's bear.

"That sounds complicated," Ned said with a frown. "Any way I can help?"

Nancy nodded. "Right now you can help keep an eye on the bear."

"Sure." He chuckled. "Only you won't find me pair skating with it."

Just then Ingrid whizzed past. Nancy watched as she bent her upper body parallel to the ice, then gracefully extended her left leg behind her.

"Bravo! Bravo!" Nancy hollered and clapped her mittened hands.

Ingrid skated up to the two of them. "A spiral. It's not too hard. Would you like to learn how?"

"Sure," Nancy said. "It looks like fun."

"I'll go help the other kids with the fire," Ned said. "Now that the sun's down, my ears feel like they're frostbitten. See you guys later."

With a wave, Ned skated off. Nancy watched him cross the pond to join several other kids clustered around the fire.

"He's cute," Ingrid said, then she spun in a semicircle. "You're a good skater, so this will be easy to learn. Watch me."

Nancy watched as Ingrid executed the spiral, slower this time.

"The trick is how well you can balance yourself," Ingrid said when she skated back. Her cheeks were flushed, and she was squeezing her hands together.

"Are you getting cold?" Nancy asked her.

"Just my fingers." Ingrid shrugged. "I think my gloves got wet when I fell earlier."

"I have a pair of dry ones in my car. You'd better put them on," Nancy suggested. Digging under her coat, she reached in her jeans pocket for her car keys and tossed them to Ingrid. "I'll practice while you get them. That way I won't make a fool of myself when I perform the spiral in front of an audience."

Ingrid laughed. "Okay. I'll just be a minute."

Ingrid sped away across the ice. Nancy tried to remember the sequence of moves for the spiral. Digging in her blades, she pushed herself forward at a fast pace, then gradually lowered her torso forward while she raised her arms to the side like wings. When she was bent at an angle, she lifted her left foot about an inch off the ice.

Immediately she lost her balance. Her right ankle jutted outward, and she fell with a thud.

"Ouch!" Nancy grumbled. Then she started to laugh. Again she tried it, and again she fell.

"So much for easy." Sliding her skates under her body, Nancy raised herself into a standing position and looked toward the fire. It glowed like a neon light against the dark sky. She could see figures moving around the fire. It looked as if most of her friends had quit skating for the night and were fixing hot chocolate and hot dogs.

A brisk wind buffeted her cheeks. Where was Ingrid? she wondered. It was getting cold, and the fire looked inviting. Maybe she'd better get back, too.

Nancy was about to skate off when a faint sound reached her ears. Pausing, she turned toward the hidden cove and held her breath.

The sound had been no louder than the rustling of pine needles in the wind, but still Nancy felt sure someone had called her name.

A shiver raced up her spine. But who? And what was someone doing in the woods on the other side of the pond, so far from the other people?

"Help!" The cry was louder this time. Someone was in trouble!

With strong thrusts Nancy skated quickly toward the shore of the hidden cove. Again, the voice rang out, this time from deep within the pine trees. "Help!"

Nancy skidded to a halt. She'd heard the cry perfectly, and it sounded like Ingrid's voice!

Nancy's mind raced as she tried to figure out what was going on. Had Ingrid's attacker followed her to the party at the pond? Had he watched her skate over to the parking lot? When he saw she was alone, had he dragged her into the woods?

Nancy took off toward the shore, her eyes intently searching the trees for some sign of movement. Suddenly she heard a zinging noise radiating from her skates. Her heart stopped beating as she recognized the sound. Before she could react, the ice cracked beneath her, and Nancy plunged into the freezing cold water!

7

Bess Is Missing!

Nancy screamed as loud as she could. With a numbing jolt the freezing water hit her legs, then her stomach. Instinctively she threw out her arms, hoping to catch on to solid ice before she fell all the way into the frigid water.

With a painful whack her left arm hit a broken edge. Nancy clawed the ice with her mittened hands, trying frantically to find something to hold on to. Then she screamed again, knowing she had to summon help quickly.

Answering shouts reached her ears.

"Hurry!" Nancy cried. She tried to pull herself onto the shelf of ice, but her skates felt like concrete blocks. Tears stung her cheeks as she slowly slipped backward.

"Nancy! Grab my wrist!" Suddenly Ned's face was about two feet from her own. He was lying on the ice, hand outstretched. He grabbed her right

59

wrist. She heard voices and saw a line of kids behind him. They flattened themselves on the ice, holding on to each other in a chain.

When he had a good grip on Nancy's wrist, Ned yelled, "Pull!"

Inch by inch Nancy was dragged across the shelf of ice.

"Hang on tight, Nancy," Ned encouraged. "Just a few feet more."

Nancy heard a slurping noise as she was pulled all the way out of the water. Digging the points of her skate blades into the ice, she forced herself as far from the hole as she could. When Ned gave one last tug and pulled her out of danger, a cheer rose from the line of kids.

"Come on, you've got to get up and moving," Ned urged.

Nancy felt strong hands grab her shoulders and lift her to her feet. She stumbled forward. Her toes were numb and her legs tingled. From the waist down, she was soaked to the bone.

Ned propelled her toward the roaring fire. Ingrid ran up to them, a look of horror on her face. "Nancy! Are you all right?"

Nancy clutched her friend's wrist. "Are *you* all right?"

Ingrid looked puzzled. "What are you talking about?"

"Talk later," Ned said firmly as he steered Nancy off the ice. Awkwardly she hobbled to a log and sat down by the crackling fire.

Without a word Ned began unlacing her skates. Someone brought a blanket and draped it over Nancy's shoulders. Her teeth chattered and she was shivering. Already, her pants legs were freezing into stiff boards.

"I've . . . got . . . extra . . . clothes . . . in . . . the car," Nancy stammered between chattering teeth.

"Good." Ned slid the socks off her bare feet, then began to rub them briskly. He looked up at her, worried. After a few minutes he stood up. "It feels like they're warming up." After Nancy got her boots on, Ned said, "Now you'd better get those wet clothes off."

"I'll help," Ingrid offered, standing up next to him. "It's all my fault—I never should have left you alone."

Nancy looked at her curiously.

"What happened, anyway?" Ned asked as he helped Nancy to her feet. "Why did you skate toward the cove? You know this pond—the ice is always thinner over there by the woods."

"I wasn't thinking," Nancy admitted. "I heard someone cry for help—the cry came from that grove of pine trees." Nancy halted and looked at Ingrid. "But it sounded just like *you*."

"Me?" Ingrid exclaimed.

"Yes. I was afraid maybe the guy who attacked you outside the shop the other night had followed you here," Nancy said, again walking toward the car.

Ingrid shook her head emphatically. "No. I stopped to warm my hands by the fire, then I went to get the gloves out of the back of the Mustang. That's when I heard you scream, and saw everybody rush across the ice toward the cove."

"Where are your dry clothes?" Ned asked when they reached the car. Nancy pointed to the trunk. "There's a suitcase in there—I'm spending the night at Bess's."

Ned took the key from Ingrid and opened the trunk. Ingrid helped Nancy unbutton her coat. Even though the top half was dry, the bottom was wet and beginning to freeze.

When Nancy slipped off her coat, Ned gave her his own jacket to put on. He had a down vest on, so Nancy knew he would stay warm. Then he handed her dry jeans and some wool socks.

"Thanks," Nancy smiled gratefully. "I'll meet you by the fire in a minute."

With a nod he strode off. Nancy unzipped her pants, then sat sideways on the front seat of the Mustang. She was too cold to worry about privacy. Besides, all the other kids were huddled by the warm fire.

"Let me help," Ingrid offered.

"Thanks, I'll need it." Nancy's jeans were so stiff, Ingrid had to yank hard on the cuffs to pull them off. For a second Nancy rubbed her bare legs, then she slid on the jeans and socks.

"Lucky you had extra clothes," Ingrid said.

"Hey, why don't I fix you a mug of hot chocolate?"

"Good idea," Nancy replied. "I'll be over in a second."

After Ingrid left, Nancy wrapped Ned's coat tighter around her, trying to quell the last of the shivers. Closing her eyes, she rested her head a minute on the back of the seat.

Had the cry for help just been her imagination? No, Nancy decided. She'd distinctly heard it.

Suddenly Nancy's head popped up and her eyes snapped open. Where was Bess? In all the confusion Nancy hadn't seen her friend.

Everybody knew Bess had the bear. What if the call for help had been a trick to lure Nancy away from Bess and the bear?

Quickly Nancy swung her legs from the car and stuck on her boots. When she stood up, her toes still felt numb, but as she ran toward the group of kids, the feeling slowly flowed back into them.

Ned was standing by the fire, talking to a friend.

"Ned!" Tugging on his arm, Nancy pulled him away from the others. "Where's Bess?"

Ned's eyes widened. "I don't know. I haven't seen her since . . ." He inhaled sharply. "Oh, no! You don't think she's the one who screamed for help?"

Nancy shook her head. "No, it wasn't her

63

voice. But I do think that somebody lured me over to the cove on purpose! And when I fell into the water, it was a stroke of luck for that person, because everybody's attention was on me."

"Which meant he or she could go after Bess and her bear without anyone seeing them," Ned finished Nancy's thoughts.

Nancy nodded tersely, then began looking around. "Come on. We've got to find her. I have a feeling our intruder the other night followed Bess here and just waited for the opportunity to get that bear."

Ned put his hand on Nancy's arm. "Wait a second, you're right except . . ."

But Nancy didn't wait to hear the rest of Ned's sentence. Frantically she strode up to the dozen kids around the fire. Ingrid was just pouring a packet of hot chocolate into a cup of water.

"Bess is missing!" Nancy told them. "We've got to look for her. Ingrid, you and Jason head toward the picnic grounds. Annabel, you and Marie check the playground area. Ralph . . ."

Quickly the pairs headed off. Several teens went back to their cars for flashlights. Others drove from the parking lot to check the park road.

Nancy grabbed Ned's hand. "Come on. Let's check out the cove. I'll stop and get my flashlight from the glove compartment."

Holding hands, the two jogged to the parking

lot. When they'd retrieved the flashlight from the Mustang, they hurried up the park road, then cut across the snow-covered grass toward the far end of the lake. There were no clouds in the sky, and the grove of pine trees loomed ahead of them.

Nancy aimed the flashlight beam on the snowy ground, searching for footprints. But there were too many tracks to tell them apart.

When they reached the dense grove of pines, Ned took the flashlight from Nancy and led the way. About twenty feet in, all tracks stopped.

"I'd say this is a dead-end clue," Ned said.

"That's for sure." Nancy blew out her breath in frustration. "If something's happened to Bess, I'll never forgive myself. I should've watched her like a hawk. I knew someone was after that bear."

Ned put his arm around her shoulders as they walked back out of the woods. "Let's get back to the others. Maybe they found Bess warming up in someone's car. And don't worry about the bear, because—"

Just then someone shouted their names. Ingrid was waving from the parking lot. Cupping her hands around her mouth, she yelled, "No one's found her anywhere!"

Nancy waved to show Ingrid she'd heard, then turned to Ned with a worried expression.

"If Bess doesn't show up in the next thirty minutes, we better call the police," Nancy said. "Usually they won't do anything for twenty-four hours. But if I contact Officer Brody, I think he'll investigate right away because of the break-in the other night—"

Suddenly Nancy heard a soft moan. "What's that?" she whispered, swinging her head in the direction that the noise came from. There was a group of blue spruce growing by the side of the road at the entrance to the parking lot.

"What's what?" Ned asked.

"I heard something, in there." Dashing over to the trees, Nancy squatted down and pushed aside a prickly branch. In the middle of the closely clustered pines, a dark lump was sprawled on the ground.

Nancy flicked on the flashlight. She caught her breath when the beam illuminated a dark blue jacket and red-striped cap.

"It's Bess!" Nancy gasped. "And it looks as if she's hurt!"

8

A New Suspect

Ducking her head, Nancy crawled between the boughs of the spruce tree. Needles scratched her face and poked her skin, but she didn't stop until she was beside Bess.

Her friend was lying on her stomach, her arms flung out over her head. Quickly Nancy checked for any sign of injury.

"Nancy?" Ned called. "Should I call nine-one-one?"

"Yes. No! Wait a minute," Nancy added as Bess suddenly moaned and rolled onto her back. Bess's eyes flew open, and she stared at Nancy.

"Bess, are you all right?" Nancy asked gently.

"All right?" Bess repeated slowly. "Yeah, I think so. What's going on?" Bess raised herself up on one elbow and glanced around, confused. "Where in the world are we?"

"Underneath some pine trees," Nancy explained.

Just then the boughs parted, and Ned peered in at them. "Is Bess okay?"

"No!" Bess winced and clapped her hand to her forehead. "My head hurts."

Nancy carefully felt Bess's head and neck. "No bumps or cuts," she reported.

"It's more like a pounding pain inside my skull," Bess said, rubbing her temples.

Nancy's eyes widened. Ducking her head, she sniffed at Bess's mouth.

Bess jerked back. "What are you doing?"

"Checking for chloroform," Nancy answered.

Bess gasped. "Now I remember! I heard a footstep on the asphalt of the parking lot. Then someone came up behind me and slapped something over my nose."

Nancy nodded. "I can smell faint traces of the chloroform, and you're acting a lot like Dotty did the other night."

"I'd better go tell the others that we found her," Ned offered, crawling from under the trees.

Nancy stopped him. "Give us a minute, Ned. If someone is out there watching, I don't want him or her to know yet that we found Bess." Sitting back on her heels, she turned to Bess. "Now tell me exactly what happened and *when* it happened."

Bess knit her brows. "Well, I was thinking how

68

good those cookies I brought would taste. They were in the Mustang, so I headed to the parking lot. Then I realized the car was locked. I turned to go back to the fire, and that's when I heard somebody come up behind me."

"Did it happen before I screamed?" Nancy asked.

"Before *you* screamed?" Bess repeated. "That was you? What happened?"

Nancy waved away her questions. "I'll tell you later. The important thing is that you did hear me scream."

"I heard a scream," Bess recalled, "but I thought it was just some of the kids fooling around. Then a couple of seconds later, whammy, I was gassed."

"What are you getting at, Nancy?" Ned asked.

"I'm wondering if the person in the trees could've called for help," Nancy explained. "Then when I skated toward the cove, the person rushed back here in time to attack Bess and steal the bear."

"Oh, but the attacker didn't get the bear," Bess said. "I got nervous when you were out there skating with Ingrid, so I gave him to Ned."

Nancy's mouth dropped open. She glared at Ned. "You had it all this time and didn't tell me?"

"I tried to tell you a couple of times," Ned protested. "But we were both so busy trying to find Bess. Actually, I don't have the bear anymore. I'd stuffed it under my jacket, and when I gave my coat to you, I locked the bear in the trunk."

"Thank goodness." Nancy smiled in relief. "Sorry if I jumped all over you."

"That's okay." Ned smiled back. "You've been through a lot—falling through the ice—"

"Nancy fell through the ice?" Bess cut in.

"It's a long story." Nancy sighed, then put her arm under Bess's shoulders. "Come on. Let's get back to the bonfire."

Together, Nancy and Ned helped Bess crawl out from beneath the spruce trees. Then Ned sprinted ahead to tell Ingrid and the others that Bess was safe.

"Boy, my legs feel a little wobbly," Bess said when she stood up.

"Where were you when you were chloroformed?" Nancy asked.

With a frown, Bess glanced around. "Let's see." She walked about ten steps down the hill toward the parking lot. Nancy's Mustang was parked at the end of the first row of cars.

"I was walking toward your car," Bess pointed. "When I remembered it was locked, I turned around about here"—Bess spun on her heels—"and started to head back."

"Stop right there," Nancy instructed. Bess halted beside the front fenders of a souped-up van and a small foreign car.

Head lowered, Nancy paced around the vehicles. "Someone could easily have hidden behind one of the cars and jumped you when you went past," she mused.

"But wouldn't one of our friends have seen the attacker?" Bess asked.

Nancy shook her head. "By then everybody was rushing out to save me. I just wish our mystery person would've left some clue. Though my guess is it's the same person who broke into the shop and your house."

"Nancy! Bess!" Ingrid called, jogging through the parking lot. "Are you all right?"

While Ingrid made Bess retell her story, Nancy continued to walk around the cars, then went over to the spruce trees.

The attack on Bess proved that Nancy's hunch was right—her friend's bear *was* the target. But why? Had Arnold lied about its not being the antique one?

Nancy pictured the little man in her mind. Somehow she couldn't imagine him creeping around in the snow attacking people. And he didn't have a big enough foot to have left the tracks at the Marvins' house.

Abruptly Nancy halted. Larry O'Keefe was a big man. And he was often around the shop—he could have watched Dotty turn off the alarm system. Getting a duplicate key to the display case would have been easy for him, too.

Larry did have an alibi, though. That's why Nancy hadn't suspected him before.

But what if Larry was working with someone? Someone who knew the bear business—like Arnold?

Nancy ran over the events in her mind, testing this new theory. The night of the robbery, Larry could have given the keys to Arnold, then made the delivery run to set up his alibi for that night. Arnold could have broken into the shop, chloroformed Dotty, and stolen the bears. And if Bess hadn't discovered the one in his shop, no one would have been the wiser.

"Nancy?" Bess's voice cut into Nancy's thoughts.

"Huh?" Nancy turned toward her two friends. Ingrid and Bess were staring curiously at her.

"I called your name about five times," Bess said.

"Oh, sorry. But I think I've figured out who stole Dotty's bears!" Nancy said excitedly. "Come on. We've got to call Officer Brody!"

"I'm actually glad Officer Brody wasn't around last night," Bess said the next morning. "My head was pounding so hard, all I wanted to do was go home and go to bed."

"Yeah." Nancy was driving Bess to work before going on to meet Officer Brody at the police station. "But I'm glad Officer Jackson came. At least she was able to write down all the details of what happened last night."

"I don't know," Bess replied. "Officer Jackson acted as though she thought we were crazy."

Nancy laughed as she pulled the Mustang in front of Beary Wonderful. "Our stories did sound pretty far out. Say hi to Dotty for me, and tell her I'll contact her as soon as I talk to Brody."

"Will do. And say hi to Ned when you see him at lunch." Bess opened the car door, waved, then swung the door shut.

Fifteen minutes later Nancy was in Officer Brody's cubicle, sitting next to his desk. Brody was talking on the phone. When he slammed down the receiver, his face was even redder than usual.

"Tough case?" Nancy inquired.

"No. The lousy garage wants two hundred bucks just for a tune-up on my car. Now"—he leaned across the top of the desk—"what's this about Bess being chloroformed? Officer Jackson gave me the report, but it sounded like a plot for a B movie."

Nancy chuckled, then summarized all that had happened. She told him her theory that the person had lured her away in order to get Bess's bear.

"In fact, I think I know who stole the bears," she added. "Larry O'Keefe and Arnold Smythe." She outlined her reasons.

"Hmmm." Brody thought for a moment. "So you still think all the crimes are tied together?"

Nancy nodded. "Unless you know something I don't."

"No," Brody admitted. "In fact, we don't have much evidence at all. The store had been wiped clean, so we couldn't get any prints.

"It appears that the stolen bears were worth more than Mrs. Baldwin's insurance policy," he added grudgingly. "And her shop is doing well, so money doesn't seem to be a motive. Still, that doesn't mean she didn't cook up a plan to sell the bears *and* collect on her policy."

"What about that bear Bess found in Arnold's shop?" Nancy leaned forward in her chair. "Have you checked that out yet?"

"No, but I'm picking up Mrs. Baldwin in twenty minutes to pay an unexpected visit to Smythe's shop," he said. "We'll see if she can identify any of her bears. I'll also check Smythe's alibi for the night of the robbery."

"Oh, good," Nancy piped up. "I'd love to come along. I need to talk to Dotty anyway."

"Wait a minute." Brody frowned. "I didn't invite you."

"But just think how much help I can be," Nancy pointed out. "I could go with Dotty to Totally Toys—that would create less suspicion than if she walked in with a police officer."

Brody reluctantly agreed. "But just remember," he warned Nancy, "Mrs. Baldwin is still a suspect. For all we know, *she* could be in cahoots with Arnold Smythe. So don't tell her anything that might blow the case."

"Right," Nancy said solemnly.

It was almost eleven when Nancy and Dotty stopped outside Totally Toys. "Oh, I just hope Arnold's not involved," Dotty said anxiously, twisting a handkerchief in her hands. "We've known each other for years!"

Nancy cast a sideways look at the shop owner. Was Dotty nervous because she *was* in cahoots with Arnold, as Brody had suggested? Was that why he'd been so casual about displaying the bear?

Nancy took a deep breath, hoping the thoughts rambling around in her head weren't true. She liked Dotty, but she also knew that Brody was right—Dotty was still a suspect, and Nancy intended to watch her and Arnold carefully.

When Nancy and Dotty stepped into Totally Toys, Arnold Smythe looked at them in surprise. Then he smoothed his balding head and, with a smile plastered on his lips, rushed over to Dotty.

"My dear, what a lovely surprise," he said, taking Dotty's hand between his palms.

With an icy smile Dotty withdrew her hand. "I'm here with my assistant to look at some of your toys," she said. "We're checking out the competition, as they say."

"Help yourself." Arnold swept his hand in the air, but Nancy thought he looked flustered.

When the bell over the door tinkled and Officer Brody walked in, the little man's mouth dropped open.

"What's going on?" Arnold asked. Dotty was leaning over, poking inside the dollhouse where Bess had discovered her bear.

"This is what's going on!" Dotty declared. Straightening, she thrust the small white bear in Arnold's face. "You're the thief who stole my bears!"

9

Caught in the Act

Arnold stared at the bear Dotty held as if he'd never seen it before. "I don't understand," he stammered.

"I think you do," Officer Brody stated. He stepped up to Arnold and grasped his upper arm. "You're under arrest for the—"

Suddenly Dotty gasped. Nancy turned and saw the older woman pull a brown bear from behind a pyramid of blocks.

"Harry!" she exclaimed as she clutched the bear to her chest. "This is Harry," she repeated to Nancy, "the bear my father gave me for winning the spelling bee in sixth grade!"

Dotty whirled and glared at Arnold Smythe. "These are my bears!" she accused. "How could you have stolen them? I thought you were my friend!"

Arnold's face had turned white. "But I didn't steal them."

"Then why don't you tell us where you were Tuesday evening at about five o'clock?" Officer Brody demanded.

"I, uh . . ." Arnold stammered, then his gaze dropped to the floor. "I closed the shop about three o'clock because of the snow, so I was home."

"Alone?" Nancy asked.

Arnold nodded, and his shoulders slumped. "But I swear I didn't steal your bears, Dotty."

With a snort of disbelief, Officer Brody tightened his grasp on Smythe's arm. "Nice acting, buddy, but the evidence speaks for itself," he said, grinning triumphantly. "Well, Detective Drew, thanks to you and Bess, we've caught our thief. Mr. Arnold Smythe, you have the right to remain silent. . . ."

Nancy watched Arnold as Officer Brody read him his rights. The little man's expression was totally confused. He kept looking over at Dotty, who was searching the shop for more of her bears.

Was Smythe acting? Nancy wondered. Or had he really not known about the bears?

When he was finished, Officer Brody handcuffed Smythe, then reached for the phone. "I'll have a search warrant here in half an hour," he told Dotty. "Then we can check out the back rooms and office."

78

"But there's nothing back there," Arnold said in a pitiful voice. "I'm telling you, I didn't steal those bears."

With a sigh Dotty went up to him. "Then what are they doing in your shop?" she asked.

Arnold shook his head in bewilderment. "I don't know."

For the next ten minutes the three sat in silence while Brody finished making several calls. Then he turned to Nancy. "An officer from the Ardmoore police station will be here any minute. Dotty needs to stay, but you may go."

Nancy nodded. If she hurried, she could just make her lunch date with Ned.

But when she finally did meet Ned at the restaurant, Nancy couldn't concentrate.

"Nancy." Ned waved a hand in front of her face to get her attention. "Is something wrong with your sandwich?"

"Hmmm?" Nancy looked up at him, then down at her tuna sandwich. She hadn't taken a bite. "No, it's fine." She flushed. "I'm sorry. I'm not being very good company. It's just that . . ."

Ned chuckled. "Look, Nancy, Arnold Smythe wouldn't be the first criminal who acted innocent."

"I know," she conceded. "But he seemed so . . . confused. I expected him to have a slick story and an airtight alibi, but he didn't."

Ned set down his soda glass. "Weren't you the one who thought Arnold was guilty?"

"Yeah." Nancy sighed and absently bit into her sandwich. For a second she chewed slowly. "Well, at least now we can eliminate Dotty as a suspect. That leaves Larry O'Keefe. He *did* have a convincing alibi." She plopped her sandwich on the plate. "Ned, how about going out with me tonight?"

Ned raised one brow. "Are you asking me for a date, Nancy Drew?"

She laughed. "Not exactly. I'm asking you to help Bess and me check out Larry O'Keefe."

"Sure, why not?" Ned grinned. "There's nothing like coming home from college for the holidays *and* a mystery."

"We didn't find any more of my bears," Dotty announced when Nancy and Ned arrived at Beary Wonderful to pick up Bess. "Officer Brody even had a search warrant for Arnold's house."

Dotty sighed, plopped her elbows on the counter, and rested her chin on her palms. "I just can't believe he did it," she added.

"Of course he did it," Bess scoffed. She was packing a large bear in a gift box. Ingrid had left for the day. "Let's just hope Arnold confesses and you get your bears back."

"Dotty, tell me more about your delivery guy, Larry," Nancy prompted.

"Larry?" Dotty asked, curious. "Why do you want to know about him?"

"Nancy has a hunch that Arnold and Larry were in on the theft together," Bess said.

Ned crossed his arms. "Actually, I'd say it was more than a hunch. It makes sense."

Nancy told Dotty all her reasons for suspecting that Larry and Arnold were partners.

"Oh, my." Dotty plucked at a gray curl. "But Larry's been working here for ages. I can't imagine . . . wait a minute. About three weeks ago he asked me if I'd lend him a thousand dollars."

"Did he say why he needed it?" Nancy asked.

Dotty shook her head. "No. I didn't press him about it, either. I just told him no. He borrowed money from me last spring and never even tried to pay me back."

"What do you think he needed the money for?" Ned asked.

Dotty shrugged. "Money problems—Larry's always getting in over his head financially. He's a good soul, just not real practical." She glanced back and forth at Nancy and Ned. "That makes Larry sound pretty guilty, doesn't it?"

Nancy cocked her head. "Not necessarily," she said. "But needing money is a pretty strong motive, especially if Larry knew Arnold could get a good price for the bears. What we really need is some proof."

"Larry's delivering several bears to a client in Chicago this evening," Bess noted. "He'll be gone until late. Maybe we can check out his apartment."

Nancy grinned at her friend. "Good idea. Can we get his address from you, Dotty?"

"I guess so." Dotty went back to her office.

"What exactly do you have in mind, Nancy?" Ned asked when Dotty left.

"If Larry needs money, he must have a reason," Nancy speculated. "Maybe he gambles, or maybe he lives way above his means. It's a good bet that we could find something in his apartment—a bank statement, IOU, credit card bill—that might tell us more about him."

"I say we just check out his apartment for the bears!" Bess declared.

Nancy laughed. "Those, too. Plus, I'd like to see if Larry has any boots in his closet with diamond-patterned soles."

Dotty bustled through the curtain and showed Nancy a page in her address book. "Apartment two-oh-two, Building B, River Heights Apartments," Dotty read out loud.

"Thanks, Dotty," Nancy said, writing down the address.

"Larry was bragging the other day about how he lives in the new singles complex," Bess told Nancy, rolling her eyes.

"Now you three be careful," Dotty cautioned as Bess put on her coat and they headed for the door.

"We will," Ned replied. "I'll make sure of it. I'm only home for two more weeks, and I'd like to enjoy what's left of my vacation."

Twenty minutes later Nancy parked the Mustang in front of Building B. It was the second group of apartments in the new complex. The drive was horseshoe-shaped. In the middle was a swimming pool, closed now for the winter. Building B was at the top of the horseshoe.

"So what's the plan?" Ned asked from the passenger seat.

Nancy had switched off the motor, and already the car was getting cold. Outside a brisk wind blew, and even though it was only six o'clock, the sky was black. The weather report had predicted snow.

Ducking down, Nancy peered out the windshield. Balconies jutted from the front of the building, two on each side. Thick bushes grew under them.

"I'll run up to the main door and find out where his apartment is located," Nancy said. "Then we'll figure out the easiest way to sneak in. At least there aren't many streetlights," she noted, "and the complex seems pretty deserted."

"That's because anyone with brains is eating a yummy dinner in their cozy house," Bess grumbled from the backseat.

"It looks as if it's going to snow any minute," Ned added, shivering.

With a chuckle Nancy opened the car door. "Hang in there, you two tough guys," she teased. "I'll only be a minute."

She shut the car door, then jogged up the steps into the main foyer. A white strip on the mailbox for apartment 202 read L. O'Keefe. She took the stairs two at a time. The door on the right had a cheery Christmas wreath hung on it. The door on the left was bare except for the numbers 202.

Striding to the left-hand apartment, Nancy checked the doorknob. Since the apartment complex was built recently, she figured the doors would be equipped with deadbolts. The sliding door to the balcony would probably be much easier to get in.

But how could she get up there without anyone seeing her? Nancy wondered as she went back outside. Frosty air stung her cheeks. If she was going to break in, she'd better do it now. Once it started snowing, she'd leave too many tracks.

"Okay, guys, it looks as if the sliding door to the balcony is the only way," Nancy said, climbing back into the car.

"Are you serious?" Bess asked. "It's in plain sight of the parking lot. Anyone driving in will see you."

"Let's hope no one does drive in," Nancy stated. "And if they do, Bess, your job is to flick on the car lights."

"What good will that do?" Bess asked.

"It will warn me to hide," Nancy explained.

"Besides, the headlights will shine on the apartment opposite Larry's, drawing the driver's attention that way."

"Pretty smart, Nancy," Ned said. "And I suppose you want me to keep lookout in the bushes."

Nancy grinned. "And boost me up to the balcony, of course."

"What kind of car does Larry drive?" Ned turned in his seat to speak to Bess. "We'll need to keep our eyes out for him."

"He might be driving the shop's van, which is tan and says Beary Wonderful on it," Bess said. "His own car is a beat-up, blue foreign thing."

Ned nodded, then flipped up his jacket collar and opened the car door. "Any other instructions, Boss?" he asked Nancy in a teasing voice.

"Yeah." She punched him lightly on the arm. "Don't drop me!"

"Do you think you can get in the apartment?" Ned called softly up to Nancy a few minutes later. He was crouching behind a bush at the side of the balcony. He'd just boosted Nancy up over the railing and onto the balcony.

Bending low, Nancy peered at the apartment's sliding glass door. There was no curtain over the window, and she could see the inside latch.

"I think I can get in using—" she began.

Just then, bright lights were reflected in the glass as a car pulled into the parking lot. Nancy snapped her head around. A shiny new Jaguar was pulling in next to the Mustang.

The Mustang's lights flashed on. Nancy ducked and flattened herself against the outside wall of the building. She crossed her fingers. If whoever got out of the car looked upward, he or she would see her right away.

The door of the Jaguar opened, and a man stepped out. Through the balcony railing, Nancy could see him from the waist up.

The man was tall, with wild, curly hair and a red scarf around his neck. Nancy's breath caught in her throat.

It was Larry O'Keefe!

10

Just in Time

Quickly Nancy flattened herself on the floor of the balcony. But she knew that if Larry O'Keefe looked up, he'd be able to see her.

And what about Ned? she wondered. Had he been able to hide?

"Be-e-e-p." Nancy heard a car horn honk once.

"Larry? Is that you?" Bess shouted plaintively from the Mustang. "My car won't start. Can you help me?"

"Your car won't start?" Nancy heard Larry say. The rest of his words were muffled by the loud honking.

Raising her head, Nancy peeked over the edge of the balcony. Larry had turned and was heading toward the Mustang.

It was now or never. Crawling like a caterpillar, Nancy made her way to the railing. She glanced at the Mustang to make sure Larry wasn't looking up at the building. Then, jumping up, she climbed over the railing.

Hanging on to the railing, Nancy lowered herself over the balcony's edge, then dropped to the snow-covered grass.

A hand reached out from the bushes and grabbed her arm. "Get in here," Ned whispered, tugging at Nancy's coat.

She scrambled into the space between the bushes and the apartment building. Ned pulled her close so that they were well hidden behind the evergreen boughs.

"That was a close one," Nancy whispered.

"Thank you again, Larry," Nancy heard Bess call out a few seconds later. There was no reply. Footsteps rang out on the concrete steps. Through the leaves Nancy glimpsed Larry's coat as he went into the apartment building.

"Now!" Ned whispered, and the two took off for the Mustang. Bess had the doors open. Nancy dived into the driver's side the same instant Ned jumped into the passenger seat.

"Boy, you guys!" Bess exclaimed from the backseat. "I thought you'd be caught for sure."

Nancy turned the key and started the motor. "Me, too," she said breathlessly. "That was quick thinking, Bess, to distract Larry like that."

Turning in his seat, Ned looked at Bess with a puzzled expression. "But wasn't Larry a little suspicious when the car *did* start right away?"

"He did look at me as if I was a total idiot,"
Bess said, laughing. "But I told him it was my
friend's Mustang and I wasn't used to driving a
car with a stick shift." She giggled. "When that
Jaguar drove up and Larry climbed out, I almost
died!"

Nancy glanced over at the Jaguar as she backed
out her Mustang. She noticed that the car had
temporary license plates, a good sign that Larry
had just bought it.

"I didn't know what to do," Bess continued.
"So I honked the horn to get his attention, and
then it popped into my mind to pretend that the
car wasn't starting."

Ned laughed, then turned back to Nancy.
"Well, our big break-in was a bust. We'll never
find out if O'Keefe has the bears stashed in
there."

"Or whether Larry wears boots with patterned
soles," Bess added.

"True, but it wasn't a total waste," Nancy said
as they drove away from the complex. "The fact
that Larry O'Keefe is now driving a Jaguar tells
us plenty."

"Right," Bess agreed. "He definitely doesn't
make that kind of money driving a delivery
truck."

"So you think we have proof that he's in
cahoots with Arnold Smythe?" Ned asked Nancy.

"Maybe," Nancy replied. "Or what if Larry
pulled off the theft all by himself?"

Bess shook her head. "No way. He has an alibi for the night of the theft—he was making a delivery in Bingham, remember? Besides, we found those two bears in Arnold's shop."

"Which is something that continues to puzzle me," Nancy thought out loud. "Why would Arnold leave the bears in plain sight? He doesn't seem stupid. Maybe somebody else put them in his store—to frame him."

Ned furrowed his brow. "Wait a second. Now you're saying Arnold *isn't* guilty? That it was all Larry?"

Nancy pursed her lips. "It's an idea. Remember how I said that Arnold didn't act as if he knew what was going on when Dotty found her bears?"

"But, Nancy," Bess said, "what did you expect him to do—confess?"

Nancy was thinking intently. "I'm going to call Officer Brody," she decided, nodding toward a service station up ahead. "I want to find out what happened when they interrogated Arnold Smythe."

She pulled in and stopped the car beside a pay phone. After jumping out, she dialed Brody's home number. When he picked it up on the third ring, Nancy could hear his TV blaring in the background.

"What do you want?" Brody asked. He didn't sound glad to hear from Nancy, but when she told him about Larry O'Keefe's Jaguar, his interest picked up.

"Whew," he whistled. "Those babies cost about ninety thousand dollars."

"About the same price as Dotty's Happy Birthday Bear," Nancy pointed out. "So what did Arnold have to say?"

"Nothing," Brody said. "He stuck like glue to his story that he didn't steal the bears. He'll be out on bail by tomorrow."

"Hmmm. Maybe that's good," Nancy mused. "He might make a move that would lead us to the other bears."

"Hey, Miss Drew," Brody reminded her. "You leave the police work to the professionals."

"Um-huh," Nancy said, not listening. "But it couldn't hurt to double-check Larry O'Keefe's alibi. So long!" Nancy hung up.

"Where are we going?" Bess asked when Nancy got back into the car.

"Bingham," Nancy replied, starting the car and driving purposefully toward the highway. A light snow was beginning to fall, and she flicked on the wipers.

"Bingham?" Ned and Bess chorused.

"We're going to retrace Larry's route the night of the robbery to see how long it took," Nancy announced. "We can pick up some food at a fast-food place, then eat on the way. My treat."

After they'd pulled into a drive-through eatery and gotten their food, Nancy checked her watch.

"Seven o'clock," she stated. "Larry said he left the shop at four-thirty and arrived in Bingham a little before six."

"Right. It took him longer than an hour because of the snow," Bess added as they pulled out onto the highway.

Ned peered out the passenger window. The flakes were falling faster and heavier. "Then we have the same weather and traffic conditions for our experiment." He glanced over at Nancy's speedometer. "But you're driving just under the speed limit—what if Larry drove faster than that?"

"Good point." Nancy sighed. "Still, we'll make the trip and just see how close we come to his time."

Two and a half hours later Nancy pulled the Mustang in front of Beary Wonderful. It was closed.

"That was an exhausting trip," Bess groaned from the backseat.

Stretching his cramped limbs, Ned added, "Well, we proved that Larry could *not* have hit Dotty over the head at five o'clock and still made it to Bingham and back by seven."

"Yeah." Nancy slumped in her seat. "And Dotty was certain of the time because of the cuckoo clock."

Suddenly Bess leaned forward over the back of Nancy's seat. "You know, it *is* a strange coincidence that Dotty just happened to lose her watch that day."

"Why?" Nancy spun around to look at her friend.

"Because Dotty's careful about things like that," Bess said. "She's very organized and punctual, and she always has that watch on."

Nancy raised her eyebrows. "How easy is it to change the time on that cuckoo clock?" she asked Bess. "To make it chime earlier?"

"Real easy—you'd just push the minute hand ahead," Bess explained.

Ned was staring at Nancy. "Now what's cooking inside that head of yours?"

Grinning with excitement, Nancy grabbed Ned's arm and gave it a squeeze. "Thanks to Bess Marvin, I think I just solved this case!"

11

Sight Unseen

Bess and Ned exchanged puzzled glances.

"You solved the case because I told you about the cuckoo clock?" Bess asked in a bewildered voice.

Nancy nodded emphatically. "What if it *wasn't* a coincidence that Dotty lost her watch? What if Larry deliberately took it?

"At four-thirty he came in to say goodbye to Dotty," she went on eagerly. "What if he only pretended to leave? He could've sneaked back into the shop and turned the hands of the clock so they'd chime five. Dotty was back in her office, so she wouldn't have seen him."

"She just would've heard the cuckoo go off five times!" Bess exclaimed.

"Then Larry went in and chloroformed her, stole the bears, changed the clock back to the correct time, and made his delivery?" Ned asked.

Nancy nodded. "Dotty had no idea how long she'd been knocked out, and we didn't get there until five-thirty—long after he'd left."

Bess raised her eyebrows. "Do you think Larry's smart enough to figure all that out *and* pull it off?"

"That's a good question," Nancy said. "But if Larry is a desperate criminal, he could be capable of just about anything!"

"What do you mean, 'desperate enough to do anything'?" Bess asked.

Nancy glanced at Ned, then at Bess. "If he's the one after your Happy Birthday Bear, next time he might use force to get it, instead of chloroform."

"Oh." Bess sucked in her breath. "It's good we left Bear in your dad's safe," she told Nancy.

Ned ran his fingers through his brown hair. "It's a good thing I hid the bear under my jacket yesterday at the pond. Bess might have been hurt if someone tried to get it away from her."

"Now the question is, how are we going to prove Larry's our guy?" Nancy asked.

"Uh-oh." Ned and Bess exchanged worried glances.

"Somehow I think that answer's going to involve a stakeout," Ned told Bess.

She nodded. "Right. And guess who Nancy will want to help her?"

"Us!" the two chorused. Nancy had to laugh, because they were right.

"Thanks for letting me spend the night at your house, Nancy," Bess said as Nancy drove her to work early the next morning.

"I just want you and Bear to be safe," Nancy said. "Especially since your parents won't be back until Sunday." She parked the Mustang along the street, then climbed out and locked it. She wanted to ask Dotty some questions before she and Ned spent the day tailing Larry O'Keefe.

Ned strode up the sidewalk, whistling. His hands were shoved in the pockets of his parka. The air was crisp and cold, and his breath puffed out in frosty clouds.

"I parked my car in the back lot, like you suggested," he told Nancy. "It's ready for a high-speed chase or a long, boring stakeout."

Nancy laughed. "Good. Larry probably knows my car, but I don't think he'll recognize yours."

When the three teens walked into the shop, Dotty was bustling around with a feather duster.

"Good morning," she greeted them. "And how was your night?"

"Boring," Bess answered. "We drove to Bingham and back in the snow."

Dotty stopped dusting. "Oh? Was there a special movie or party in Bingham?"

Ned chuckled. "No, Mrs. Baldwin. When you

96

go out with Nancy, you usually spend the night hunting for clues."

Dotty smiled. "And did you find out anything new?"

Nancy nodded. "Maybe. Tell me about your lost watch, Dotty."

"Oh, it's not lost anymore," Dotty explained. "I found it yesterday behind the sink."

"May I see it?" Nancy asked.

"Of course." Dotty trotted into the back room.

"If she's got the watch, that means Larry didn't take it," Bess said.

"Here it is," Dotty said, returning with a silver watch in her hand. She showed it to Nancy. "It must have fallen off my wrist—see how the clasp is broken?"

Taking the watch, Nancy walked over to the front window to study it in the sunlight. The metal clasp looked flat, as if someone had pounded it with a hammer.

"What are you looking for?" Ned asked, peering over her shoulder.

"I'm not sure," Nancy murmured. She looked up at Dotty. "Do you ever take the watch off while you're in the shop?"

"Only when I clean my bears," Dotty answered. "Sometimes I get an antique bear that's really dirty. It's a very delicate process, because you can't get water on the bear, so—"

"When was the last time you cleaned a bear?" Nancy interrupted.

Dotty thought a minute. "Let's see. It must have been Monday afternoon."

Bess's eyes widened. "That's the day before the robbery!"

"Come on. I want you to show me where you found the watch." Nancy led the shop owner to the bathroom. Ned and Bess followed them.

The bathroom had a toilet, sink, a shelf for supplies, and a trash can.

"I set my watch on the shelf over the sink," Dotty recalled. "Then I made up a solution of Woolite liquid. That's how you clean the bears— you work the Woolite into a foam, then dab it on the fur with a damp washcloth. I was just finishing when you came into the shop, Nancy, to pick up Bess."

"And when did you go back to get the watch?" Nancy asked.

"Well, Ingrid had that run-in with the mysterious attacker Monday night, remember? In the excitement I forgot all about my watch. And then on Tuesday I was the only one in the shop, so I was pretty busy until it began to snow. And then, of course, the store was robbed."

Bess and Nancy gave each other knowing looks.

"So you think that Larry attacked Ingrid that day, and then came into the shop and swiped the watch?" Ned asked Nancy.

"It would've been the perfect opportunity," Nancy agreed. Stepping from the bathroom, she noted that the back door was only a few strides away. Larry could have been in and out in a few seconds.

"Was Larry in the store Monday?" Nancy asked. "Could he have seen the watch on the shelf?"

"Yes," Bess chimed in. "He came in late that afternoon to pick up his paycheck."

"You three are jumping to conclusions," Dotty protested. "I found my watch behind the sink. It obviously fell off the shelf and got kicked back there."

Nancy tilted her head. "I don't know. Look at this clasp." She held up the watch. "Maybe someone stepped on the clasp, but I doubt it. It looks as if it was hit with a hammer. Somebody wanted to make sure you weren't wearing this watch."

Suddenly the back door of the storeroom opened, and Larry O'Keefe stepped into the shop. With a puzzled expression he stared at the four people standing in the bathroom and its doorway.

"Thanks again for showing me how to clean my bears," Nancy quickly improvised.

Taking her cue, Bess reached up and pulled the bottle of Woolite off the shelf. "Oh, hi, Larry," she added, as if she had just noticed him.

"Hey." Larry nodded once, then walked toward Dotty's office. "You had some packages that needed mailing today?"

"We'd better be going," Nancy told Dotty.

"Bess, we'll pick you up at five." After waving goodbye, Nancy and Ned hurried from the shop.

"Come on," Nancy urged as they headed for the back parking lot. "Let's get to your car. This may be our best chance to tail Larry."

Ned and Nancy just had time to shut the car doors when Larry walked out the back door of the shop. A delivery van was parked behind it.

"First stop, post office," Ned predicted as he started his car.

"Right. But it's the second stop I'm interested in," Nancy said.

Driving from the parking lot, Nancy and Ned followed the van to the post office, careful not to get too close. Larry parked and went inside, carrying several boxes.

When Larry finally came out, Ned pulled his car from its parking space and tailed the van down Heights Street at a safe distance. It wasn't long before the van turned onto the highway.

"What should we do now?" Ned asked. "The guy could be headed for Chicago, for all we know."

"Keep following him," Nancy said. "Ardmoore is in this direction, too."

"Ardmoore?" Ned asked.

"That's the town where Arnold Smythe has his store, Totally Toys," Nancy said.

"Do you think Larry's headed for the shop?"

Nancy crossed her fingers. "Let's hope so. It might be the break we're looking for!"

An hour later, at the exit for Ardmoore, Larry left the highway. Nancy squeezed Ned's arm excitedly as they followed the van. Larry drove down Ardmoore's main street and pulled up in front of Totally Toys. Then he got out and ran up the sidewalk into the shop.

Ned cruised slowly past the store. A sign hung on the front door that said Closed.

"Closed in the middle of the morning?" Ned questioned.

"My thoughts exactly." Nancy nodded. "I have a feeling Larry flipped that sign around to make sure no customers dropped in. I wonder if the store has a back entrance."

Ned stepped on his brakes. "Oh, no—you're not going in there. Remember, you said Larry O'Keefe must be desperate by now."

"But I *have* to find out what's going on between those two," Nancy said firmly. "I promise I'll only sneak in and listen. If I'm not out in fifteen minutes, you can burst in and rescue me."

"Okay," Ned reluctantly agreed.

Ned made a right-hand turn and drove into an alley running parallel to the main street. The back doors of several shops opened into the alley.

"Totally Toys must be about the fourth shop down," Nancy guessed. She spotted a small bear sign on one of the back doors. "There it is."

"I'll find a place in front to park," Ned said. "And remember, if you're not out in fifteen minutes, I'm coming in."

Nancy nodded, then jumped from the car. She tried the doorknob, and it turned easily. Waving at Ned to go, she opened the door and quietly slipped inside the shop.

The back room was dark. Nancy slowly closed the door behind her, then held her breath. She could hear the murmur of voices coming from the front of the shop.

When her eyes adjusted to the dark, she looked around. Arnold's storeroom wasn't quite as junky as Dotty's, but still there were boxes everywhere. A tall pile was stacked by the door leading into the front. Nancy decided to move closer and hide behind the stack. That way she could hear what Larry and Arnold were discussing.

Cautiously Nancy picked her way through the crowded storeroom until she reached the boxes. There was a narrow space between the stack and some metal shelving. Nancy wedged herself into the space, then held her breath.

Larry's voice was louder but muffled, and she couldn't hear Arnold at all. Then she noticed a vent about two feet over her head. Light from the other room streamed through the slats.

If only she could get closer to it.

The boxes! Nancy cautiously lifted the top box from the stack and set it on the ground. Standing on it, she peered down through the slats. She could only see the top of Larry's head, but she could hear them both—perfectly.

"Look, Smythe," Larry snarled. "You'd better have fifty thousand dollars for me in one hour. Otherwise, I'll go right to the police and tell them about your shoddy schemes against Dotty. And with all the other evidence against you, they'll put you in jail forever!"

12

Cross and Double Cross

Schemes against Dotty? Nancy repeated to herself. It didn't sound as if Larry was just talking about the theft. Was Arnold doing something else illegal?

Abruptly Larry turned on his heels, stalked to the front door, and opened it. "One hour!" he growled to Arnold. Then he left, slamming the door behind him. The bell on the door jingled crazily, so that Nancy couldn't hear Arnold's angry words.

Nancy stepped off the box and quietly exhaled. This wasn't the proof she was hoping for. She'd expected to witness an exchange of bears or money or something. But hearing the encounter between the two men had only confused the case.

It sounded as though Larry was trying to blackmail Arnold for something other than the theft. Otherwise, wouldn't Larry have said, "I'll tell the police that you stole the bears"? What "shoddy schemes against Dotty" was he speaking of?

Two things were certain, Nancy thought to herself: One, if Larry and Arnold had been partners, they had turned on each other. And two, Arnold was guilty of *something*.

If Larry was trying to blackmail Arnold, that might make Arnold desperate—maybe even desperate enough to confess the whole story to someone else.

Taking a deep breath, Nancy walked toward the front of the shop. This could be the perfect time to get Arnold to talk. She knew she was taking a risk, but Ned was outside ready to burst in if anything went wrong. Besides, Nancy had tackled tougher opponents than pudgy Arnold Smythe.

Still, her heart beat rapidly as she stepped through the doorway. Arnold was sitting on a stool behind the counter, staring down at his glasses.

"Hello, Mr. Smythe," Nancy spoke. Arnold Smythe's head snapped up. "I'm Nancy Drew—remember? I was here with Dotty Baldwin yesterday."

"What are you doing here?" he asked, jumping off the stool. "How did you get in?"

She nodded toward the back room. "It wasn't locked. I sneaked in and overheard your conversation with Larry O'Keefe."

"Larry?" Arnold's gaze flew to the closed front door. "Uh, you must be mistaken. He hasn't been here for weeks."

Crossing her arms, Nancy stepped closer to him. "No, I'm not mistaken," she said firmly. "I followed him here, all the way from River Heights."

Arnold frowned and ran his fingers across his bald head. Then with a groan he slumped onto the stool. "So why don't you call the police and tell them everything you overheard? It's better than trying to scrape up fifty thousand dollars to pay Crazy Larry."

"What are you paying him for?" Nancy asked.

He shot her a weary look. "I heard that policeman yesterday call you a detective, but believe me, this is none of your business."

"But I think we can help each other," Nancy urged him. "I don't believe you stole the bears. I think Larry's the culprit, and I want to nail him."

With a sigh Arnold adjusted his glasses, then slowly stood up. "You're just a kid," he said, sounding defeated. "There's no way you can get me out of this mess."

"Try me," Nancy challenged.

Arnold gave her an appraising look, then abruptly said, "All right—I haven't got anything to lose. Larry wants me to pay him to keep quiet about . . . about some dishonest things I did with him. He figures if he goes to the police with this information, it'll nail me for good." Arnold winced. "And he's right."

"What dishonest things?" Nancy pressed.

"Well, I . . ." Arnold hesitated. "I occasionally paid Larry for information about Dotty's business deals. You see, people from all over the world call her when they're trying to sell special toys or collections. Larry could pick up their phone numbers and names—even how much money Dotty was offering them. Then I . . ." He blushed and glanced down at his hands.

"Then you'd offer the people a little more money and buy the stuff yourself," Nancy guessed.

He nodded. "I know it wasn't right, but I've always loved the challenge of getting something that I knew other people wanted."

Nancy furrowed her brow. "Would you go so far as to steal from that person?"

Looking shocked, Arnold straightened his shoulders. "I'm a businessman, not a thief!"

"Then how did the bears get into your shop?" Nancy asked.

Arnold shook his head. "At first I really didn't know," he confessed. "But when I thought about it later, I realized Larry must have planted them. I distinctly recall him coming here Wednesday morning. He said Dotty was thinking about selling her Happy Birthday Bear, and he wanted to know how much the bear was worth.

"He could've easily slipped the bears into my displays when I wasn't looking," Arnold concluded sheepishly. "He probably wanted to cast suspicion away from him. And it worked."

Crossing her arms, Nancy paced across the floor. "Did you tell all this to the police?"

"I told them Larry was in the shop and could have planted the bears," Arnold said. "But I think they assumed I made it up to get myself off the hook."

"Let me ask one more question," Nancy said. "The day my friend Bess and I brought in the Happy Birthday Bear, were you telling us the truth? Or was it really the antique bear?"

"It's not antique—it has plastic eyes. I told you that," Arnold insisted.

"Hmmm." Nancy thought a minute. She'd hoped to learn who could be after Bess's bear. But there was no time to worry about that right now. They needed to catch Larry O'Keefe.

"I guess our next step is to trap Larry into revealing that he has Dotty's bears," Nancy suggested. "He'll need a buyer for them, right?"

"Right," Arnold agreed. "And since every dealer and collector in the state knows that the Happy Birthday Bear is Dotty's, it won't be easy to sell it—or the rest of the bears, for that matter."

Tilting her chin, Nancy looked at Arnold. "Then I think *you'd* better offer to buy them—instead of paying him the hush money."

Arnold looked interested. "Oh—I like that idea. Then when he hands them to me, you'll nail him, right?"

"The police will nail him," Nancy corrected. "Let's call Officer Brody—"

Suddenly the bell on the front door jangled shrilly. "All right! Hands on your head, Mr. Smythe!" a voice ordered.

Nancy spun around. Ned was standing in the doorway, his hands raised in a karate stance.

"Good heavens!" Arnold exclaimed.

Clapping her palm over her mouth, Nancy tried to hold back a giggle. "It's all right, Ned. Mr. Smythe and I have decided to work together to catch Larry O'Keefe."

Ned looked relieved. "That's good. I wasn't looking forward to a brawl."

"Don't speak too soon, Ned," Nancy said, smiling grimly. "I have a feeling Larry O'Keefe isn't going to give up without a fight."

She turned back to Arnold. "Now, let's figure out what a good price would be for those thirteen bears. Then you can call Larry and set up a meeting."

"Why do we always get the job of hiding in cramped, stuffy rooms?" Ned whispered to Nancy.

She smiled. "Because we're detectives."

The two were in the back storeroom of Totally Toys, sitting on several boxes under the vent where Nancy had eavesdropped earlier. Ned and Nancy had stacked a high wall of boxes in front of them, in case Larry came into the storeroom.

When Arnold had called him, Larry had protested that he hadn't stolen the bears. But then Arnold said he'd pay one hundred and fifty thousand dollars for the Happy Birthday Bear and the other twelve. Larry said he would come right over.

Immediately afterward, Nancy called Officer Brody and told him to be at the shop, too. Then the teens helped Arnold put together a shoebox that would look as if it was full of cash. It was filled with newspaper strips, with a layer of twenty dollar bills on top. Nancy hoped it would fool Larry long enough to make him give the bears to Arnold.

Nancy checked her watch. It was fifteen minutes after one. Larry had said he'd be at the shop at one-thirty.

"I'm starving," Ned whispered. "We never had any lunch."

Nancy jabbed him with her elbow. "I can't believe you can think about food at a time like—"

Suddenly the shop bell jingled and the front door flew open. Nancy jumped up on a box and peered through the slats in the vent.

Larry O'Keefe slammed the door shut behind him, flipped over the Closed sign, then strode toward the counter. His red scarf flapped behind him, and his gray-streaked hair looked more tousled than usual.

"So what's this great deal you want to make?" Larry said to Arnold. "That is, *if* I have the bears."

Nancy stood on tiptoes and peered downward. She could just see the top of the counter. The shoebox sat in the middle of it. Arnold's hands were on either end, gripping it tight.

"I-I've decided if I'm going to be tried for s-s-stealing those bears, at least I ought to have them," Arnold stammered.

Larry snorted. "That sounds like a mighty fishy story to me. You got cops in here?"

Nancy crouched down beside Ned on the boxes.

"Uh, no, Larry," Arnold replied. "Why would you think that? All I want to do is buy those bears. If you must know, I have a very hot buyer. But he wants them *now*. He won't stick around and wait for the police to get their hands on the bears first."

Nancy heard Larry grunt. Cautiously she and Ned both stood up and peered through the vent.

"So where are the bears?" Arnold asked. "You do have them, don't you?"

"You think I'm going to tell you that right away?" Larry snorted. "Not until I see the money!"

Nancy groaned. This wasn't going the way she'd hoped. Larry had come early, and he hadn't brought the bears with him. What if he decided he wanted the money *and* the bears? He could easily swipe the shoebox from Arnold and run.

Ned nudged Nancy. "Where's super-cop Brody?" he hissed, a worried frown on his face.

"I don't know," Nancy whispered back.

Below her, Arnold was still arguing with Larry, trying to get Larry to show him the bears. "You listen carefully to those two," she told Ned softly. "You may have to be a witness. I've got to snoop through Larry's car and see if I can find those bears before it's too late."

Ned nodded and silently squeezed her arm.

Nancy stole through the storeroom to the back door. After inching it open, she slipped outside.

The bright sun made her blink. Shading her eyes, she glanced around the alley. Larry had entered through the front door, but she saw that he had parked in back. She immediately recognized the delivery truck from Beary Wonderful.

Nancy raced over to the van. If Larry got suspicious of Arnold's deal, or decided to steal the money, he could be out any second.

The van wasn't locked. After opening the driver's side door, Nancy climbed in. Several boxes were piled in the back. Nancy slid between the two front seats. Hunching down behind the driver's seat, she grabbed the first box.

It was sealed shut and addressed to Beary Wonderful. Excited, Nancy pulled her penknife from her purse and quickly cut the tape. What better place to hide stolen bears than in a shipment of bears!

When she opened the box and folded aside the packing, a row of identical stuffed brown bears stared up at her. Nancy dug her hand deeper into the box and grabbed one from the bottom.

This one was cream colored and had a raggedy-fur face. Nancy felt one of the eyes. It was cold and smooth.

A glass eye! She'd found one of Dotty's antique bears!

Nancy dug deeper into the box and lifted out a larger, snow white bear with dreamy eyes. The Happy Birthday Bear!

"Now we've got you, Larry," Nancy said to herself as she pawed through the box.

Just then the driver's door was yanked open. Nancy crouched silently against the back of the driver's seat.

Peering up, she could see the back of Larry's head as he settled grumpily into the seat.

With an angry curse he slammed the door shut and started the motor with a roar. The next second Nancy was almost thrown to the floor as the van zoomed forward. She braced herself against the back of the seat.

Larry's making a getaway, Nancy thought wildly. And she was trapped inside the van!

13

Trapped!

Nancy grabbed for something to hold on to as the van careened down the alley.

"Stop!" She could hear Ned yelling outside.

Suddenly Larry's hand reached down by her shoulder. Nancy watched him drop the shoebox on the van floor, then push it under the passenger's seat.

He'd stolen the money!

Nancy clapped her hands over her mouth, suppressing a cry. Think calmly, she told herself. Ned knows where you are. He'll get the license plate number and call the police.

R-r-r-r. The sound of a police siren reached her ears. Officer Brody!

Speeding up, the van made a sharp turn, throwing Nancy against the side. The siren was right behind them, closer and more insistent.

Larry muttered something, then began to slow down. Nancy breathed a sigh of relief.

Gravel crunched as the van pulled off the road and stopped. Larry rolled down the window.

"Is something wrong, Officer?" he asked politely.

"You were speeding, sir—fifty miles an hour in a thirty-mile speed zone," the officer replied.

Nancy's heart sank. It wasn't Officer Brody!

Thinking quickly, she began to bang on the side of the van. "Help!"

"What in the world?" Larry sputtered, twisting around in his seat. When he saw her, his surprised expression changed to anger. "What're *you* doing in here?"

"Help!" Nancy screamed again. She jumped up and ran for the back doors of the van. "Oh, no!" Nancy cried when she saw there wasn't any handle. The doors were locked from the outside!

"What's going on in there?" Nancy heard the policeman's confused voice. Frantically she pounded on the back doors.

"You're trapped now!" Larry growled. He slid from his seat and lunged toward her. Spinning around, Nancy pressed her back against the doors and faced him.

Then she heard a second siren's wail. Tires screeched as another car pulled up behind the van.

Still Larry came toward her, his arms outstretched and his fingers bent into claws. He looked ready to strangle her. Nancy took a deep breath. When he was a foot away, she kicked out, hitting him square on the jaw.

It only stopped him for a second.

"Let me out!" Nancy screamed. Then Larry's fingers were around her throat.

Suddenly the van doors flew open. Nancy toppled backward, dragging Larry with her. They fell in a heap on the ground.

Larry still didn't let go, and Nancy fought for air. With both hands she grabbed his wrists and dug her fingernails into his flesh.

At the same time two police officers seized Larry's arms from behind and pulled him off Nancy. In the blur of motion Nancy recognized Officers Brody and Jackson. Then she doubled over, gagging and coughing.

Officer Brody slammed Larry against the side of the van while Officer Jackson handcuffed him.

Then Brody helped Nancy to her feet. "Are you okay?" he asked.

She nodded, then pointed to Larry. "That guy not only stole Dotty's bears," she gasped, "he stole Arnold's money."

"I did not!" Larry lunged toward Nancy. Grabbing the cuffs, Officer Jackson yanked him back. "She's trying to frame me!" Larry yelled.

"Get O'Keefe out of here," Brody told his partner. "Read him his rights and put him in the squad car."

116

"Let me go," Larry demanded as Officer Jackson led him away. The policeman who'd stopped the van for speeding took his other arm, and the two marched him to the squad car.

"Nancy!"

Nancy turned and saw Ned jump from his car. When he reached her, he threw his arms around her shoulders and hugged her.

"That was a close one," he said. "When I saw Larry drive off with you in the van, I thought you were a goner."

"Me, too." Nancy sighed. "But it was worth it. Look at this!" She led Ned and Officer Brody to the back of the van.

Nancy reached inside and pulled one of the boxes toward her. "Larry had several of Dotty's bears hidden in here," she said. She dug out a bear and held it up. "And he has the shoebox of money stashed under the front seat."

"It looks as if we have enough evidence to put O'Keefe in jail for a long time," Officer Brody said. "I'll have Mrs. Baldwin come down to the police station and identify her bears. We'd better get a statement from Mr. Smythe, too."

"Is Arnold all right?" Nancy asked Ned.

He chuckled. "Fine. When Larry threatened to punch him, Arnold handed over the box without another word. It's good Larry didn't get a chance to count the money. He would've been furious if he saw it was mostly newspaper."

Nancy shuddered. "Not as angry as when he turned around and saw me."

Ned pulled her tight against him. "Come on. After Brody gets our statements, let's go get a late lunch. You deserve it!"

"So the mystery's finally solved," Bess said. It was five o'clock, and Nancy and Ned had arrived at Beary Wonderful to pick their friend up.

"And Larry *was* the thief," Ingrid added from the front of the shop. She shook her head. "I never would have figured he was clever enough to pull it off."

It was almost closing time. Ingrid was sweeping the floor while Bess was at the cash register, totaling receipts. Nancy stood next to her, her elbows propped on the counter. Dotty was still at the police station, verifying that the stolen bears were hers.

"Oh, he was clever, all right," Ned said. "He really had the police fooled with his alibi." Ned had squeezed his big frame into a child-size chair used in one of the displays, and his legs stretched into the middle of the shop.

"So your theory about changing the time on the cuckoo clock was correct," Bess said as she punched numbers into the calculator.

Nancy shrugged. "I guess so. When I called Officer Brody, though, he said Larry hasn't confessed to anything. He's still claiming I planted the bears in the back of his van."

"I hope the police don't believe the crook!" Ingrid exclaimed as she walked toward the counter.

"They don't," Nancy confirmed. "Arnold, Ned, and I all had the same story, so it isn't likely they'd believe Larry's lies." Nancy frowned. "Brody says Larry hotly denies having anything to do with breaking into the Marvins' house or assaulting Bess at the pond. Or with assaulting you here on Monday night, Ingrid. We have proof that he stole the bears, but there's no evidence to tie him to those other events. That bothers me."

"I think we ought to celebrate," Ingrid broke into Nancy's train of thought. "Why don't you guys come to my house for dinner tonight?"

"We'd love—" Bess started to say, but Nancy jabbed her in the side.

"We'd love to, but Ned got three concert tickets to see this hot new band," Nancy said quickly. "We have to be at the coliseum at seven and won't be home until late. How about dinner tomorrow night?"

"Uh, sure," Ingrid replied, but Nancy could tell she was hurt. "I'll check with my parents." Ingrid reached under the counter and pulled out her purse. "I'd better go. I have to open the shop in the morning. Bess, do you mind waiting until Dotty gets here to lock up?"

Bess smiled. "Not at all. Sorry we can't come for dinner tonight."

119

"That's okay. See you." Ingrid waved, then left through the back of the shop.

When Bess was sure her friend had gone, she turned to Nancy. "Ned doesn't have concert tickets. Why did you lie to Ingrid?" she demanded. "Ingrid's my friend and you hurt her feelings."

"I know, Bess, and I'm sorry," Nancy apologized. "But I don't think the mystery is solved. My gut feeling is that someone else is after your bear. But if we're going to catch that someone, we need to lay a secret trap—nobody should know about it, not even Ingrid or Dotty. And I'd like to start tonight."

"Wait a second," Ned said, leaning forward in his chair. "You're saying Larry isn't responsible?"

"Right. Brody said Larry had an airtight alibi the night Bess was assaulted," Nancy explained. "About twenty people saw him all night at a pool parlor. Besides, why would Larry go after Bess's bear? It isn't all that valuable, and his only motive is money."

"Maybe he thought it was the real one," Bess suggested.

"But do you want to take a chance?" Nancy pressed Bess. "What if you're alone and someone does go after Bear?"

Bess glanced nervously at Nancy, then at Ned. "I guess you're right. What should we do?"

"Tonight, the three of us will hide out at your

house, Bess," Nancy laid out her plan. "We'll make it look as if no one's home. Then maybe whoever's after your bear will try to break in."

"Only we'll be waiting!" Bess added gleefully.

Nancy shivered. The temperature outside had dropped, and even though she was wearing Ned's goosedown vest under her coat, she was still cold.

It was ten o'clock, and Nancy was huddled behind the bushes by the Marvins' back porch. The first time the intruder had broken in, he had used the back door. Nancy had a hunch he would try the same thing again. She and Ned had taken hour shifts. Ned was stationed now in the living room, while Bess was pretending to be asleep in her bedroom.

Nancy wiggled her toes inside her fur-lined boots, then checked her watch again. She'd wait about twenty minutes longer, then give up.

Just then a movement caught her eye. Parting the bushes, Nancy looked into the Marvins' backyard.

Someone was climbing over the fence!

The intruder jumped to the ground and turned toward the bushes where Nancy was hiding. She saw a ski mask pulled down over the person's face.

It has to be the same person, Nancy thought excitedly. And this time I'm going to get him!

Crunching through the snow, the figure crossed the yard to the Marvins' back porch. I'll wait until he breaks into the house before going after him, Nancy thought. That way there would be no question of guilt.

When she raised herself to a crouching position, a twig stabbed her in the cheek. She flinched backward, and her bootheel slipped on a patch of ice.

Whoosh! Nancy's foot slid out from under her. She grabbed at some branches to keep from falling.

The same second the intruder heard Nancy in the bushes. The person spun around, jumped down the steps, and raced through the snow toward the back fence.

"Ned! Bess! He's out back!" Nancy yelled before taking off. She sprinted through the snow after the fleeing figure.

Reaching the back fence, the intruder paused to swing a leg over. Nancy made a flying tackle. With all her strength she grabbed the person's waist and twisted sideways, pulling them both onto the ground.

The back porch lights flicked on. Nancy straddled the intruder's chest. Then she reached down and ripped off the ski mask.

Blond hair tumbled from underneath the mask. Nancy jerked back in surprise.

It was Ingrid!

14

The Missing Piece

"Ingrid!" Nancy exclaimed, jumping off her friend. "What in the world are you doing here?"

"Ingrid?" Bess and Ned chorused as they ran up behind Nancy.

Propping herself up, Ingrid glared up at the three of them, then fixed an angry gaze on Nancy. "What in the world are *you* doing hiding in the bushes?" she demanded. "You scared me half to death!"

"I'm sorry." Nancy grabbed Ingrid's gloved hand and helped her up.

"I told you this was a dumb idea, Nancy," Bess grumbled. She didn't have a coat on, and she clutched the Happy Birthday Bear, dressed in a nightshirt. "Look who we caught!"

Nancy studied Ingrid for a second. "Maybe Ingrid needs to explain why she was here so late when she thought we were at a concert?"

"If you must know, I figured you guys would be home from the concert by now," Ingrid explained. "I was coming over to tell you that I'm leaving for Germany a day early. My flight on Sunday was canceled, so I booked another flight for tomorrow morning at five A.M. I'll fly from River Heights to Chicago, then pick up my international flight from there."

Bess shot Nancy an I-told-you-so look and said, "See? Now doesn't that make sense?"

"It would make even more sense for all of us to go inside," Ned said. "It's freezing out here."

"You're right," Nancy agreed. "Hot chocolate, anyone?"

The four teens trooped into the Marvins' kitchen. While Nancy and Ingrid took off their snowy clothes, Bess and Ned made hot chocolate.

"I'm glad you came over, Ingrid," Bess said. "Otherwise, we wouldn't have been able to say goodbye."

"I'm glad, too. Even if I did get tackled." Ingrid laughed as she sat down at the kitchen table. "Now, why don't you guys tell me what you were doing hiding in a dark house?"

"It was Nancy's idea—let her explain it." Bess jerked her thumb at Nancy.

Nancy handed Ingrid a mug of hot chocolate, then took a sip of her own drink. "I still think someone besides Larry is after Bess's bear," she explained. "I was hoping if the person thought no one was home, he'd break in again."

"I get it." Ingrid nodded. "I think."

Ned laughed. "Don't worry. Unless you hang around with Nancy all the time, this detective stuff can get confusing."

The three girls laughed, then everyone chatted until Ingrid had to go home.

"Guard that bear carefully," Ingrid said as she slipped on her coat. "In all the confusion I never did get the one from Arnold."

"That's too bad." Bess patted Ingrid's arm sympathetically. "Dotty will probably get another order soon. If you're still in Germany, I'll send it right to you."

"Or maybe you can buy one in Germany," Nancy suggested.

"Maybe." Ingrid murmured as she gazed wistfully at Bess's bear. "But it will be too late for my cousin's birthday."

"Why don't Nancy and I walk you home?" Bess suggested. "Ned can guard Bear." She handed the stuffed bear to Ned, then reached for her coat.

"Good idea." Nancy grinned. "It is a beautiful night—I should know since I spent almost an hour freezing in it."

The teens all laughed. Ingrid waved goodbye to Ned, then the three girls headed out the back door. About fifteen minutes later the two girls had dropped Ingrid at her house and were walking up the Marvins' back steps.

"Do you think I should have given my Happy

125

Birthday Bear to Ingrid?" Bess asked as they went in the back door.

"No." Nancy shook her head. "You've gotten pretty attached to him." She slipped off her coat and draped it on a kitchen chair. Suddenly she grabbed her friend's wrist. "Shhh," she whispered, putting a finger to her lips. "I hear someone talking. And it's not Ned!"

Bess shut her mouth. Nancy held her breath, straining to listen. It sounded as if Ned was talking to someone in the living room. He could be listening to the radio, Nancy thought, or he might be on the phone, but it didn't sound like either one.

Nancy opened the middle kitchen drawer and quietly took out a rolling pin. Then, motioning for Bess to stay put, she tiptoed down the hall.

When she reached the entrance to the living room, Nancy flattened herself against the hall wall. Then she peered cautiously around the doorframe.

A tall man wearing a black coat was standing three feet in front of Nancy, his back toward her. Ned was directly behind him, so Nancy couldn't see the expression on Ned's face. But one thing was for sure—the man held Bess's bear tucked under his arm!

He was tall enough to be Ingrid's attacker, Nancy judged. Quickly she glanced down at his feet. He had rubber galoshes pulled up over his shoes. Nancy could bet there was a diamond-patterned grid on the sole!

Raising the rolling pin high, Nancy strode into the living room. "Put your hands in the air and don't move," she ordered, "or I'll whack you. Quick, Ned, check to see if he has a gun."

"But, Nancy—" Ned began.

"Bess! Call the police!" Nancy yelled toward the kitchen. Arm still raised, Nancy stood behind the man, ready to hit him if he moved an inch. But he stood frozen in place with his arms raised.

"Nancy!" Ned said more firmly, stepping toward her. "This is a police officer."

"A police officer?" Bess squeaked as she poked her head around the doorway.

"Maybe that's what he told you," Nancy insisted. "But I bet this is the man who assaulted Bess and Ingrid. And now he's here to steal Bess's bear!"

"No, Nancy," Ned said emphatically. "This is Kommissar Franz Schmidt of the German police force. He's got identification to prove it."

"Uh, Miss Drew, your friend is right," the man said without moving. Nancy noticed he had a thick German accent.

Nancy looked at Ned incredulously. "A police officer from *Germany?*"

Ned nodded. "And he didn't force his way in here. He knocked politely."

The man pointed to his back pocket. "Please. My papers are in my wallet," he said.

"You take his wallet out, Bess," Nancy said, still holding the rolling pin. "I'm not taking any chances."

Bess slipped the wallet from his pocket and opened it. "Uh-oh. There's a passport with his picture and everything. He really is a German police officer!"

"Let me see." Nancy sidled over to look at the passport. "ID's can be forged," she said brusquely. "Sir, we need more proof that you are a police officer."

"You are wise to be cautious, miss," the tall man said to Nancy. "Please call Chief McGinnis of the River Heights Police Department. He is the only person who knows I am here on special assignment. In fact, he suggested I come here tonight. He said the famous teen detective, Nancy Drew, was staying at the Marvins' house because of her friend's bear."

Nancy nodded. "Ned, keep watch over Kommissar Schmidt while I call McGinnis." She handed Ned the rolling pin and headed for the phone in the hall.

"Whenever I speak with him, I give him a special code word, *Meissen*," the man called out after her.

Nancy dialed the police headquarters and asked for Chief McGinnis. "Hello, Nancy," the chief answered. "Did Kommissar Schmidt find you? I told him you were a detective and could help him capture the smugglers."

"Uh, yes he did find us," Nancy stammered, suddenly feeling foolish. "He said to ask you for his code word so I'd know he was on the level."

"Right," the chief said. *Meissen*—that's the code word."

"Thanks, Chief," Nancy replied as she slowly hung up. Oh, boy, Nancy thought as she turned to face the others. First she'd tackled Ingrid, then she'd almost whacked a German police officer. She wasn't doing so well with this case.

Ned stood with his arms crossed. "Well?"

"I owe Kommissar Schmidt an apology," Nancy admitted. She held out her hand. "I'm sorry, sir. I thought you were the intruder who's been trying to steal Bess's bear."

Finally lowering his arms, Schmidt smiled and shook Nancy's hand. "That's all right," he said. "I would have done the same thing you did."

"Now, what's this about smugglers?" Nancy asked, sitting on the arm of the sofa.

"Smugglers?" Ned and Bess repeated.

Schmidt sank down into a wing chair. "I am in the United States trying to capture the members of a sophisticated smuggling ring," he explained. "Your bear, Ms. Marvin, contains a priceless Meissen figurine that was stolen from a German museum."

Bess's mouth dropped open. She sat on the sofa with a plop. "My bear has *what* inside it?"

"Meissen is a very famous type of porcelain," Schmidt filled her in. "It has been produced in

Germany, in the towns of Meissen and Dresden, ever since the early eighteenth century.

"Packed inside your bear is an exquisite ballerina that dates from 1734," he went on. "It is one of a kind. The dancer's partner, a porcelain cavalier, was stolen last year. We think he is now in the hands of a collector in River Heights, and that the ballerina is on her way to join him."

Holding her bear at arm's length, Bess stared at it. "No wonder someone's been after him."

"How did the smugglers get the ballerina inside the bear?" Ned asked, joining Bess on the sofa.

"As I said, this is a sophisticated bunch of thieves," Schmidt said. "We've been trying to crack the ring for two years. Six months ago we learned that the stolen items were leaving Germany in shipments of stuffed animals from the Otto C. Bear factory.

"We placed an undercover detective in the factory," he continued. "Our detective discovered that the export manager was placing the stolen items inside certain animals. Since these stuffed animals are all handmade, it was easy for him to slip a figurine or small vase inside before the animals were sewn up."

Bess nodded. "Those bears are certainly big enough to hide a little statue," she commented.

Schmidt nodded. "Yes, and the stuffing keeps the porcelain items from breaking. It's really quite ingenious. The manager would then contact the smugglers. He'd tell them what kind of animal the stolen item was in and where it was being shipped."

"So that's how the ballerina ended up at Beary Wonderful," Nancy said, impressed. "But surely you don't think Dotty is part of the smuggling ring?"

Schmidt shook his head. "No. We've checked her out carefully, and she seems to be innocent. But we do think some stolen items are being shipped to her store. The stuffed animals look normal, so she'd never guess something is inside them."

"That's for sure," Bess said as she turned Bear around in her hands. "He doesn't even feel heavy."

"Then the courier goes to the store where the stuffed animal was shipped and buys it," Nancy guessed.

"What's a courier?" Bess asked.

"A courier is like a go-between," Schmidt replied. "The smuggling ring uses couriers here in the United States to pick up the stuffed animals at whatever stores they're shipped to. The courier then takes the animal, with the stolen item inside, to a client who buys it."

"Later, the courier would somehow get the money back to the smuggling ring in Germany," Nancy concluded. "So that person would need to have connections in Germany." She frowned intently. Suddenly she could see the pieces of the puzzle falling into place.

"I followed the shipment to Mrs. Baldwin's store," Schmidt recounted. "Then I watched and waited to see who was going to buy it."

Bess's eyes popped open. "So one of our customers is the courier!"

"No, in this case the courier had managed to get an inside connection," Schmidt said. "She actually worked at the store."

"*She?*" Ned repeated with a puzzled expression. Bess looked speechless.

Nancy was one step ahead of them. "She works at Beary Wonderful and knows exactly when the shipments come in," she declared. "She immediately stashed Bear on the back shelf when it arrived at the shop. But when she tried to buy the Happy Birthday Bear, she found that you'd bought it, Bess. And she has wanted that bear ever since."

"Nancy! Are you accusing Ingrid?" Bess gasped.

Nancy gave a firm nod. "Yes. Ingrid Jennings is the courier for the smuggling ring!"

15

The Trail of the Courier

"Ms. Drew is right—Ingrid is the courier," Kommissar Schmidt confirmed. He nodded at Ned and Bess, who sat on the sofa staring at him with open mouths. "I've been following her the past week, hoping she'd snatch the bear."

"You *wanted* her to steal my bear?" Bess asked.

"Yes. That way I could have tailed her to the collector in River Heights," Schmidt pointed out. "We wanted to arrest Ingrid and the collector together. Our hope was that one or both of them would give us the names of the rest of the smugglers, so we could shut the ring down."

"Boy, I sure messed up your plans," Nancy murmured.

Ned chuckled. "That's true—you were doing everything possible to keep the bear from being stolen, Nan. But tell me something, Kommissar

Schmidt—were you at the pond the night of the skating party?"

Schmidt smiled apologetically. "Yes. I concealed myself in the trees. I watched Ingrid sneak around the pond and call for help. When you skated over and fell through the ice, Ms. Drew, she ran back to the parked cars."

Bess narrowed her eyes. "Where she whacked me on the head—some friend!"

"If your friends hadn't reacted so quickly, I would have blown my cover and saved you," Schmidt told Nancy. "But since I was keeping an eye on you, unfortunately I wasn't able to prevent Ingrid from getting to Ms. Marvin here."

"And Ingrid was also the one who broke into our house that night?" Bess asked.

Schmidt nodded.

"What about those big bootprints?" Ned asked.

"Ingrid was smart enough to disguise her tracks," Nancy replied. "She probably wore her father's boots." She pointed to Schmidt's galoshes. "I'll bet they were a pair similar to those, since the soles made the same pattern."

Schmidt looked down at his galoshes. "I bought these in Germany, of course. But Mr. Jennings lived in Germany, too, until earlier this year. He could easily own an identical pair."

"Then those were your bootprints in the snow that night Ingrid was attacked outside the shop," Nancy deduced.

Schmidt looked impressed. "Yes. I was tailing Ingrid. She's a new courier, but she's very clever —she spotted me that night and sneaked up on *me*. Then she cried for help, making it look as if I was the culprit."

Ned crossed his arms. "So Ingrid knew someone was onto her."

"Yes," Schmidt said, "but it was too late to get another detective on the case. I had to keep tailing her and hope that she'd be desperate enough to make a mistake. And she did—she underestimated you, Nancy. Maybe you didn't know *who* was after the bear, but you knew somebody was. And you were able to keep the bear safe."

Bess groaned. "I'll bet Ingrid came here tonight to try one last time to steal the bear."

"Do you think Ingrid is really going back to Germany tomorrow?" Nancy asked. She stood up and began pacing across the living room rug.

"Yes," Schmidt said, his eyes following Nancy. "She'll keep to her plans so she doesn't arouse suspicion. I suspect that since Ingrid failed, the ring is sending someone else to get the bear." He suddenly frowned and looked directly at Bess. "Someone who won't hesitate to use force."

"Oh," Bess said in a small voice.

Stopping in her tracks, Nancy inhaled sharply. "Then we need to make sure Ingrid doesn't fail. She needs to get the bear so you can follow her and catch the collector."

"Are you saying we should let Ingrid steal the bear?" Ned asked, surprised by Nancy's suggestion.

"No—we could offer to take Ingrid to the airport tomorrow and give her the bear as a going-away present," Nancy answered. "Bess was sort of thinking about doing that, anyway. Right, Bess?"

"Umm, well . . . yeah," Bess stammered, holding her bear close. "But if Bear gets into Ingrid's hands, I'll never get him back."

"That's right," Schmidt agreed solemnly. "But Nancy's plan might be the only way to catch Ingrid in the act of passing the smuggled goods to the collector."

Bess exhaled slowly, then stood up. "I'll give Ingrid a call," she said, going to the phone in the hall.

Two minutes later Bess came back into the living room. "It's all set," she said glumly. "Ingrid was ecstatic when I told her I was giving her the bear. We're supposed to pick her up at four A.M. and take her to the River Heights airport."

Nancy checked her watch. "That's only four hours from now. I'm not sure I'll be able to get to sleep between now and then."

"Me, either." Ned stood and stretched. "Coffee, anyone? It's going to be a long night."

* * *

"We'll see you in two weeks," Bess said, giving Ingrid a hug.

"I'll miss you guys," Ingrid replied as she picked up her carry-on bag. She gave Nancy, Ned, and Bess a sad smile.

The four young people were standing outside the security gate at the small River Heights air terminal. It was four-thirty in the morning, and the place seemed deserted.

"And, Bess, thanks again for Bear," Ingrid said, holding up the stuffed animal, which she had tucked under her arm. "My cousin will really appreciate him."

"Yeah, well, I'm sure Dotty will get another one," Bess said cheerfully.

Nancy shot Bess an encouraging smile. She knew Bess was forcing herself to be cheerful. She's doing a great acting job, Nancy thought— especially since this really was the last time Bess would ever see her Happy Birthday Bear.

With a wave Ingrid turned and went through the security gate, then disappeared down the long walkway.

"So where's Schmidt?" Ned asked in a whisper. "Isn't he supposed to be here?"

Nancy glanced around the waiting room and ticket areas. The only people there were a handful of passengers and airline clerks. "He said he would be in disguise," Nancy answered. "But maybe he's at the boarding area."

"So what do we do next?" Bess asked, yawning sleepily.

"We split up, then find inconspicuous places to keep watch for Ingrid," Nancy said.

Bess pulled a baseball cap from her purse. She plunked it on her head and tucked in her hair. "I'll go sit in the snack shop," she volunteered.

"And I'll hang around the newsstand and hide behind a sports magazine," Ned said, striding across the lobby. "See you later."

Nancy waved, then gazed around the waiting room. She spied an old newspaper lying on a plastic seat. After unfolding the paper, she sat down and held it up in front of her face as though she were reading it.

If she was right, it wouldn't be long before Ingrid came back out of the boarding area. And if the plan worked, Schmidt would be close behind her.

About five minutes later Nancy saw Ingrid at a telephone in the airport lobby. Bear was clutched tightly in her arms. That's funny, Nancy thought. I never saw her leave the boarding area. How did she get to the phone? When Ingrid's back was to her, Nancy scanned the large room, searching for Schmidt.

Where was he?

Quickly she glanced back at Ingrid. She had hung up. Had she called the art collector to confirm the meeting?

After picking up her carry-on bag, Ingrid

rushed out the double doors to the front walk. She was headed for the main parking lot.

Nancy dropped her newspaper and jumped up. Ned was already striding across the lobby.

"Where's Schmidt?" he asked urgently.

Nancy shook her head worriedly. "I don't know, but I think something went wrong. We're going to have to switch to plan B."

"Plan B?" Ned looked confused.

"Yes," Nancy said determinedly. "That's where you and Bess hunt for Schmidt, then call Chief McGinnis. I'm going to follow Ingrid. We can't lose her now!"

"Okay." Ned waved over to Bess, who was at her post in the snack shop, finishing a doughnut. "But as soon as you know where Ingrid's going, you call the police," he warned Nancy.

"I will," Nancy promised.

Nancy went out through a side door into the smaller parking lot where she'd parked the Mustang. The main exit was visible from this lot, so Nancy knew she'd be able to spot Ingrid leaving.

Five minutes later Ingrid drove a yellow rental car down the airport drive toward the exit. When the car took a left turn, Nancy pulled out from her own parking place.

Ingrid might recognize the Mustang, Nancy realized. She could only hope Ingrid wasn't expecting anyone to follow her. That just might be the case, if Ingrid had already managed to get Schmidt out of the way.

Nancy followed the yellow car down River Heights' main street and into an exclusive area on the north end of town. After making a couple of turns, Ingrid slowed down to cruise along a quiet residential street. She seemed to be checking the house numbers.

Nancy pulled the Mustang over to the curb and waited until Ingrid finally came to a stop. She saw Ingrid climb out of the car and head up a walk.

Nancy steered back into the street and drove past the house. It was a gorgeous mansion surrounded by old oaks and manicured shrubs. Nancy checked the house number, then turned around in the next driveway.

Nancy headed for a pay phone she'd noticed on a corner two blocks back. After calling the police, she was coming right back. There was no way she was going to let Ingrid get away now!

Ten minutes later Nancy was peering into the stained-glass window that framed the mansion's ornate front door. Holding her breath, she grasped the doorknob and turned. It wasn't locked. Obviously Ingrid wasn't expecting trouble.

As Nancy slipped in the door, she could hear the murmur of voices coming from down the hall. Nancy recognized Ingrid's voice. On tiptoes she made her way toward an open doorway.

The voices became louder as Nancy approached. When she peered around the doorway, Nancy saw a gray-haired woman standing in the middle of a wood-paneled library. She was holding a delicate ballerina figurine up to the light of a crystal chandelier.

Ingrid stood next to the woman, her back to Nancy. Nancy saw that Ingrid was holding a pair of scissors. A pile of stuffing and white fur lay scattered upon the gleaming hardwood floor at her feet. One brown eye stared from half a round head.

It was the remains of Bess's bear!

"It's superb!" the woman exclaimed, twirling the ballerina in her fingers.

The woman looked familiar, Nancy thought. Then she remembered—she'd seen her picture on the society page of the River Heights *Gazette*. She was Helen Wiseman, a widow who was involved with several charities — and buying stolen goods, Nancy thought ruefully.

"Now, how about the money?" Ingrid demanded.

"Oh, yes." Mrs. Wiseman pointed to a briefcase on a high-backed chair.

Ingrid strode over to the case and popped open the latches. It was stuffed full of cash. Quickly she began counting the stacks of crisp green bills.

"It appears it's all here," Ingrid stated as she locked the case back up. "Now I'm on the next shuttle to Chicago, then off to Germany."

Nancy's heart flip-flopped. Ingrid was leaving! Unless Nancy made a move, the courier would get away before the police arrived.

Reacting quickly, Nancy stepped into the doorway. "Hello, Ingrid," she greeted her coolly. "Hello, Mrs. Wiseman. I see that Kommissar Jennings got here before I did."

"What are you talking about?" Still holding the ballerina, Mrs. Wiseman stared in surprise at Nancy.

"I'm talking about you being royally tricked, Mrs. Wiseman," Nancy bluffed. *"I'm* the courier. And you just gave your money to a detective in the German police force!"

16

Schmidt to the Rescue

Mrs. Wiseman clutched her heart as she glared at Ingrid. "You're a police detective?" she asked.

"No, I—" Ingrid protested.

Nancy stepped closer. "I can prove she is!" she told Mrs. Wiseman. Nancy's voice sounded sure, though her heart was pounding. She knew she couldn't stall them forever.

Where were the police?

"She's been working undercover at Beary Wonderful all fall," Nancy stated. "That's why it took me so long to get the bear. She watches anyone who goes into the store like a hawk. I finally had to get my friend Bess to buy the bear. And—"

"No! No!" Ingrid cut in. "She's lying. She's the one who's a detective."

Striding across the floor, Nancy grasped Mrs. Wiseman's arm. "Don't believe her," she insisted. "This morning Detective Jennings pre-

143

tended to leave for Germany. I started over here, figuring this was my chance to get the figurine to you. But she tricked me. She got off the plane, knocked me out, and stole the bear!

"Then she came here, under the ruse of being the courier," Nancy finished. "I'm just glad I made it here in time to warn you."

"I . . . I . . ." Mrs. Wiseman sputtered. Her gaze shifted to Ingrid. Nancy could see the glint of suspicion in the older woman's eyes.

Nancy held her breath. Her gamble had worked! Schmidt had said Ingrid was a new courier, and apparently Mrs. Wiseman had never met her before.

"Ms. Drew tells a convincing story," Ingrid said coldly, holding the briefcase to her chest. "Now let's see her back it up. When I came in this morning, I gave you a password, Mrs. Wiseman. Why don't you ask Nancy what it is?"

Nancy's heart dropped to her stomach. How could she bluff her way out of this one?

"Of course I know the password," Nancy played for time. Then she suddenly gasped and pointed to the window behind Ingrid. "It's the police!" she shouted. "She brought the police!"

With a cry Mrs. Wiseman swung around toward the window. Nancy darted forward and grabbed the figurine from her hand. Then she held it above the hardwood floor.

"Nobody move," she warned, "or I'll smash this to a million pieces."

Ingrid only chuckled. "I couldn't care less about that piece of old china. My job's done—I've got the money." She patted the briefcase. "But I don't need for some blabbermouth witness to send me to jail."

Glancing behind her, Ingrid spotted a fire poker on the hearth and moved to pick it up. "One blow with this and you'll be out of my hair forever, Nancy Drew. Then I really am off to Germany."

Waving the poker, Ingrid advanced threateningly toward Nancy. Slowly Nancy backed toward the doorway, the figurine still in her hand. Maybe she could make a run for it.

Mrs. Wiseman gasped. "My ballerina! I've waited years for that ballerina!"

"Then tell Ingrid to drop the poker," Nancy warned.

"No way." With a growl Ingrid sprang at Nancy.

Spinning around, Nancy sprinted down the hall. Her free hand grabbed the front doorknob just as the poker whistled through the air. Nancy ducked sideways right before the metal rod cracked into the wood, just inches from her head.

Nancy twisted in time to see Ingrid raise the poker, ready to strike again.

Just then the door flew open. "Police!" someone shouted. Two officers rushed in and grabbed Ingrid's arms.

But the opening door had struck Nancy from

the side, throwing her off balance. The dancer flew from her fingers. In horror Nancy watched the figurine sail through the air.

Suddenly Kommissar Schmidt dived through the open doorway. Arms outstretched, he reached for the falling ballerina. He caught it just before it hit the hard floor.

Nancy let out her breath. From flat on the floor Schmidt grinned up at her.

"Did you think after all this I'd let it break?" he asked with a chuckle.

"No." Nancy shook her head. Then she began to laugh wildly with relief.

"Nancy Drew, I don't know how to thank you," Kommissar Schmidt said two days later. "We found more than fifty German antiques locked up in Mrs. Wiseman's vault."

The German detective was standing in the middle of Beary Wonderful, talking to Nancy, Ned, Bess, Arnold Smythe, and Dotty. Officer Brody stood next to him, his policeman's hat in his hand.

"Wow." Bess whistled. "She really was a dedicated collector.

"Yes," Schmidt said. "She had a small fortune in Meissen porcelain and Dresden glass."

"What's going to happen to Mrs. Wiseman?" Nancy asked.

"I hope she's treated as roughly as I was!" Arnold grumbled. "And I was innocent."

Dotty shot him an accusing look. "Not quite," she corrected him.

Arnold dropped his gaze. "You're right, Dotty," he admitted. "And I guess a million apologies will never be enough."

Nancy grinned at the two, then turned back to Schmidt.

"Mrs. Wiseman has cooperated fully—in return for leniency, of course," Schmidt said. "She's told us the name of the art dealer in Chicago she dealt with—Herbert Hiller. He was supposed to be very reputable. It seems collectors asked him for specific art pieces that they wanted at any price. He would then contact the smuggling ring and they would steal the pieces."

"But don't worry," Officer Brody added. "Helen Wiseman won't get off scot-free."

"What about Ingrid?" Ned asked. "I hope she's not getting off too easy—especially after she went after Nancy with that poker."

"This is Ingrid's first offense, and she has offered to testify against the members of the smuggling ring," Officer Brody said. "So she'll be given a reduced sentence, too."

Schmidt nodded. "But it's worth it. The German police have already arrested the manager at the Otto C. Bear factory. With Ingrid's testimony, it won't be long before the whole smuggling operation is shut down."

Bess sighed. "I just don't understand why Ingrid did it."

"It seems Ingrid was recruited by a boyfriend she met at the university," Schmidt explained. "He figured she'd be perfect because she had a legitimate reason to go back and forth from the United States to Germany. It was easy money, and maybe Ingrid got caught up in the excitement of being a courier." He shrugged. "We'll probably never know."

"Really," Dotty said. "And to think I was taken in by her. She knew exactly what I ordered, so it was easy for her to tell the smuggling ring what animals to place the stolen items in."

"Then the smuggling ring contacted the manager at Otto C. Bear," Schmidt added. "He was the one who actually sewed the stolen pieces inside the stuffed animals. Dotty, your shop was targeted because it was in the same town Ingrid lived in, plus you ordered a lot of animals. But we think the ballerina in the Happy Birthday Bear was the first stolen item Ingrid was involved with."

"Unfortunately, Bess bought the bear before Ingrid could get hold of it." Nancy grinned. "That sure put a glitch in her plans."

"Not really," Schmidt said. "She figured it would be a snap to get the bear back from Bess. She just hadn't counted on you, Nancy."

Ned chuckled. "Yeah, that's Nancy for you— don't mess with the best."

"I couldn't have done it without you and Bess," Nancy said.

"Thank goodness you three were there at the airport," Schmidt said. "My disguise as a maintenance man didn't fool Ingrid for a second."

Officer Brody looked at Schmidt with raised brows. "So how did Ingrid manage to knock you out and tie you up?" he asked in a teasing voice.

Embarrassed, Schmidt shook his head. "She had her own disguise on," he said. "She sneaked out of the plane and into the bathroom without me seeing her. I was sweeping the hall when someone called out from the ladies' room, complaining about an overflowing sink. When I went in, she struck me on the head with a metal towel dispenser she had pried off the wall."

"That's why I didn't see Ingrid leave the boarding area," Nancy said. "She was in disguise. And then she took off the disguise before I saw her at the phone."

"When we went to look for Schmidt, we heard a woman screaming," Bess continued. "She'd found him bound and gagged in one of the stalls. Ned alerted airport security, and I called Chief McGinnis. The security guards found Ingrid's disguise in the trash—a wig, glasses, and a floppy hat."

"Thanks to Officer Brody and the River Heights Police, I made it to Helen Wiseman's house in time to catch the ballerina," Schmidt said with a laugh. "Now Officer Brody is taking me to the airport, and I'm off to Germany to close down the smuggling ring—for good."

Brody put on his hat. "Well, Detective Drew, you outdid yourself this time. Two crimes in one week—that must be some kind of record."

"That's right!" Dotty pointed to the display case. Once again it was filled with antique bears. "I got all my bears back, and there's enough evidence against Larry to put him away for a long time. I'll be a little more careful next time I hire a delivery man." She looked hopefully over at Ned. "Have you thought about a part-time job, young man?"

Ned held up his hands in protest. "No, thanks. I have two more weeks of vacation, and then it's back to college."

Nancy and Bess laughed, then said goodbye to Kommissar Schmidt and Officer Brody.

When they'd gone, Bess sighed. "Maybe I can be your delivery man, Dotty," she suggested. "After all, I still owe you for my Happy Birthday Bear. Even though he's in a hundred pieces."

"Oh, that's right," Dotty said in a serious voice. "That adds up to a lot of deliveries."

Bess groaned, and her shoulders slumped.

Dotty's serious expression turned into a mischievous grin. "Perk up, dear. Arnold and I have something for you." She bustled into the back room.

"I'm glad to see you and Dotty made up," Nancy told Arnold.

"'Made up' isn't exactly what happened," Arnold confessed. "I had to promise to let Dotty in on all *my* hot deals. That woman drives a hard bargain. No wonder her shop's such a success."

When Dotty came through the curtained doorway, her hands were behind her back. "Arnold and I wanted to thank you, Bess," she said, holding up a white bear wearing a red ribbon.

"It's the Happy Birthday Bear!" Bess exclaimed. Then she looked at Dotty in confusion. "But I don't understand. He was ruined."

"This is the bear Arnold had ordered," Dotty explained. "And he's a gift from both of us."

Taking the bear in her arms, Bess hugged him tight. "Oh, thank you."

"And for you, Nancy," Dotty went on, "we have the start of your own Otto C. Bear collection." Drawing her other hand from behind her back, she handed Nancy a fuzzy brown bear wearing a knitted blue cap and matching scarf.

"He's adorable!" Nancy said, feeling its soft fur.

"Read the tag attached," Arnold said, pointing to the scarf around the bear's neck.

Flipping over the tag, Nancy read out loud, "To Nancy Drew—A Beary Wonderful Detective—thank you for solving the Teddy Bear Mysteries!"